DATELINE: BELGRADE

DATELINE: BELGRADE

WITH EXCERPTS FROM SELF-INFLICTED
WOUNDS: THE BALKANS TRILOGY

P. A. DUNCAN

UNEXPECTED PATHS

Printed in the United States of America.

ISBN: 979-8656106870

FIRST EDITION: August 2020

Published by Unexpected Paths.

www.unexpectedpaths.com

 Created with Vellum

For Dr. Dennis Reinhardt, who, at Madison College, first kindled the fire in me about the history of "the powder keg of Europe."

EPIGRAPH

The only thing the Balkans export is history.

— WAMU Broadcast, 1995

CONTENTS

PROLOGUE

EUROSCENE

Europe from a Modern Point of View

Vol. 1 No. 1 January 2000

Welcome to EuroScene, a new eZine for Europeans by Europeans. To subscribe, respond to this email and write Subscribe in the subject line.

Euroscene is free, but please support our sponsors. Of course, if you contribute to EuroScene, we may be able to reduce those annoying sponsor ads.

EuroScene kicks off by concentrating on the political situation in Yugoslavia. Whether Yugoslavia falls or stands, whether their elections scheduled for next year will be democratic or staged will affect the future of other countries in the European Union.

EuroScene has a correspondent full-time in Belgrade who will contribute regularly; however, to protect that correspondent from the State Security Police—not known for its support of Freedom of the Press—that correspondent's byline will not appear.

To comment on any EuroScene article, click on "Respond to the Author" at the end of each article.

We hope you enjoy EuroScene.

Editorial Staff

CHAPTER 1

An excerpt from *Self-Inflicted Wounds: Welcome to Belgrade* (Book 1)

Not long after Alexei left for White Nights, Mai gathered her cameras and recorders, intending to go cover the night's demonstrations. She pulled out her mobile to call a cab, but it rang. She recognized Ranovesic's number.

"Good evening, Commander," she answered. "What can I do for you this evening?"

"I am in a police car. On my way to pick you up."

"What have I done?"

"You, nothing. Well, unless you want to tell me what you have done."

"Absolutely nothing the Belgrade Police need to know about. I assure you."

"Okay. Someone did a drive-by on Jovan Ivanovski's house an hour ago."

Jovan Ivanovski was a prominent opposition leader, a Montenegrin, and Milošević's security services had tried to kill him a couple of times without success.

"How bad?" Mai asked.

"I'm headed to Mladenovac, Ivanovski's neighbor-hood, to find out. I thought you and your partner might want to accompany me."

"My partner is not available. Would I be going with you in my capacity as an FSB observer?"

"Of course. Look, I know Ivanovski is far from being an associate of Milošević, and this may be completely unrelated to your, uh, work, your purpose here," Ranovesić said.

"It wouldn't hurt to look into it," Mai replied. "It could be a ruse to throw us off-track. You're on your way here?" She listened to several seconds of Ranovesić's hesitant silence and reminded herself to be patient.

"That was a bit of a bluff. I have no idea where in Belgrade you are."

Mai gave him the address.

"Fifteen minutes," he said and hung up.

Not knowing what would await her in Mladenovac, Mai assumed she'd be gone the whole night. She could let Alexei wonder, a little payback for his infatuation with White Nights.

No, she was making too much of that.

Or she wasn't making enough of it.

Undecided, she wrote him a note and left it on the kitchen table where he'd see it.

☙ ☙

EuroScene
Dateline: Belgrade

Exclusive to EuroScene from the
Serbian Renewal Movement

EuroScene's Belgrade correspondent received this email (in English), and we have printed it in its entirety, with some editing for English grammar and punctuation. This article illustrates two points: Yugoslavians interested in justice do exist, and the state of affairs in that country is beyond desperate. Our correspondent has provided explanatory notes in brackets [ ]. —Editorial Staff

A Truck is the Killer

"The only way our country can emerge from its deep crisis is to follow the rule of law and assure we have democratic elections. Any other process will worsen our political, social, and economic status and lead to more civil war.

"However, the current regime isn't interested in changing Serbia by peaceful, democratic means. Its use of state terrorism is blatant, and it is anti-everything: state, nation, democracy, human. A recent attempt on the life of SPO leader Jovan Ivanovski by a Killer Truck and the murders of four prominent SPO leaders prove this.

[Note: This attempt—where a large truck ran cars in Ivanovski's entourage off a mountain road—took place last year. The police termed it an "accident," but four people *were* killed. Ivanovski escaped injury.]

"Our experts have discovered Yugoslavian Customs had confiscated the Killer Truck from its owner in 1996 and then assigned the Killer Truck to SDB [Serbian State Security]. The Killer Truck's license plate is among those on a secret registry of 'special' vehicles. A few days before the crime, the Killer Truck needed some sort of repair, which was accomplished at an auto-repair shop used by SDB, and the repair bill was paid by SDB. In Belgrade, the Killer Truck was loaded with sand bags and moved near where Ivanovski was traveling to, in preparation for the attack.

"The day after the crime, SDB members descended on the repair shop, rounded up all the workers, and threatened them unless they remained silent about repairing the Killer Truck.

"When queried, an SDB spokesman admitted the national security service had had a Mercedes truck repaired there, but they said it only resembled the Killer Truck and was not the same because it had a different serial number.

"SPO asked to see the truck resembling the Killer Truck, but we have not received an answer. Because the 'similar' truck *does not exist*. Also, someone disappeared the secret registry of SDB vehicles.

"We can come to only one logical conclusion: The Killer Truck used in the attack against SPO *does* belong to SDB.

"And the Customs Officer who originally confiscated the truck has also 'died' in a car 'accident,' one that occurred not long after the attack on SPO members *and* after an announcement that the official would be a 'key witness' concerning the Killer Truck. News of the customs official's 'accident' has not appeared on any media, which is unusual when a federal official dies.

"An ex-SDB member told us the customs official's 'accident' was clearly a political assassination. SPO believes that key witness's assassination was ordered by none other than Duško Bogdanović, SDB Serbia chief, along with the SDB Belgrade chief, who are members of YUL. [This is the Yugoslav Left Party, founded by Slobodan Milošević's wife, Mira Markovic; however, the email provides no proof they ordered the assassination of any of these individuals.]

"Foreign press have reported that the SDB is now controlled by YUL and SRS [Serbian Socialist Party], and they have turned SDB into a terrorist organization. The constitution established a Safety Board to control SDB (and all other police forces), but its meetings go unapproved. And no one has established an Investigation Board for the Killer Truck 'accident.'

"SPO believes those now controlling the SDB have planned many acts of terror, assassinations, bombings, and other crimes. In other words, the current regime is behind these criminal and terrorist acts. There is no other credible conclusion.

"From SDB come other terrorist actions: stopping democratic broadcasts on state television, arresting and abusing local functionaries and even ordinary citizens and denying them their rights, executing orders to beat students and other participants in legal protests, preparing legislation to stifle free media and free speech, fostering civil war in Montenegro, etc. Any and all of this will destabilize the entire region. This is totalitarianism, pure and simple.

"YUL and SRS push us closer to civil war at a time when we need peace and democracy for our political, economic, and national problems. SPO will fight this any way we can. We will stop state terrorism and these deadly anti-democracy events. To us, the murderers of our four brothers by the Killer Truck— Bogdanović and everyone else covering up this crime —are the true enemies. We have put them on a wanted poster. We will bring them to justice. Peacefully. Unless they make us use force.

"We will never forget or forgive. We will never be quiet. We have taken a vow for justice and for freedom. Otherwise, this regime will fill Serbian cemeteries to overflowing.

"All for justice. Justice for all."

Respond to author.

CHAPTER 2

An excerpt from *Self-Inflicted Wounds:*
***Welcome to Belgrade* (Book 1)**

The address Oleg had given her was a mid-rise office building. Most of its windows were boarded up, but Mai could hear music, something soft and pleasing. A Bach fugue, she believed. At the door, she put her hand on the butt of her Beretta and rang the bell with her left.

The door opened and confirmed the Bach but also framed a tall woman with overdone hair and exaggerated make-up. A hot-pink, floor-length negligee trimmed with black feathers swirled about her ankles.

Not a woman.

Either a transvestite or a transexual. Drago Kovač must cater to a variety of sexual preferences.

The woman looked her over. "You have the wrong place, darling," she said, her voice like a Serbian Harvey Fierstein's. "The male brothel is—"

"I'm here to see Kovač," Mai said in Serbian, "courtesy of Oleg Dmitrov."

The door opened wider, the woman stepping to one side. Mai unbuttoned her coat as she entered so any security inside would see her Beretta.

"This way, darling," the woman said and minced across the lobby.

A few customers' heads turned—Mai was still in her leather outfit—and Mai scanned her surroundings.

An assortment of women stood around or lounged about, talking to men, sharing drinks, or exchanging gropes. At first glance the women appeared to enjoy the activity, but Mai caught the disconnect in their eyes.

A thin woman wearing a leather bikini and thigh-high boots posed against a wall, one hand on her hip. Dark red lipstick outlined a sullen mouth, and kohl-ringed eyes stared at nothing. A studded dog collar was tight around her neck, and she wore elbow-length black leather gloves. In her other hand she held a dog leash, and Mai followed it to where a girl, no more than twelve, sat on the floor. The leash ended at a matching dog collar on the girl's neck. Her outfit was a grotesque imitation of the woman's, and the girl looked enough like the woman they had to be mother and daughter.

A man walked up to the woman and handed her a drink. He reached down and patted the child's head, as if petting a dog. The mother faked interest in what the man said to her, but the child's eyes showed she'd gone far beyond fear and indifference.

EuroScene
Dateline: Belgrade

Just a Commodity
(Belgrade Correspondent)
WARNING: The subject matter of this article is explicit and may be disturbing.

HAD the West been able to foresee what bringing down the former Soviet Union would cost in terms of lives and dignity, would they have systematically continued on that course?

Yes, they would have, and they would say, "The Soviets were working as hard to bring us down as we were for them."

However, the Soviets would never have succeeded because they couldn't. The massive military spending was conducted solely to address the economic and strategic power of the West, to appear to be an equal power. When the Soviet economies could bear no more, the inevitable occurred. To apply strategic language, what happened afterward was "collateral damage," a phrase the West tosses about with characteristic arrogance.

We see the pictures of the old soldiers and *babushkas*, their pensions evapourated, put out on the streets to freeze or get lead poisoning from bootleg vodka. We see the unpaid soldiers in tattered uniforms selling their services to any *Mafiya* boss who comes along, and the West shrugs. They brought it on themselves, western politicians say, with their commitment to communism.

Hidden from our eyes, however, is an age-old commodity whose supply exploded with the failing economies. Women, many of them well-educated, who in the rush to adapt to this "new Russia" or "new Bulgaria" or new whatever, ended up on the streets, too, because there are no jobs for them. The jobs that exist must go to men who support their families—the influence of the Orthodox Church and other Christian denominations seeking inroads among the former faithless. These women have become easy prey to white slavers, a term from old B movies brought into awful reality.

The Russian *Mafiya* learned well from its American and Italian counterparts, who no longer eschew prostitution but covet the profit from it. They addict these women to drugs, sell the use of their bodies to pay for their fixes, and keep the profits for themselves. Much as American plantation owners bragged about roofs over the heads of slaves and food on their tables, these modern-day "owners" of human flesh evoke charitable motivation for their prostitution of a generation of Eastern European women.

Some of it has a veneer of civilization in so-called matchmaking services. An ad in some European or American fringe magazine offering catalogues of Russian women dolled up for a photo shoot, a head and shoulders photo that doesn't show the emaciated bodies with needle marks on the arms and legs.

"Olga is 35, has a Ph.D. in applied physics and is eager for an opportunity in America."

"Tatiana is 28, studying law, looking for a companion who will support her legal training."

"Nadezhda is a 32-year old surgeon, seeking the partnership of a doctor husband with whom she can set up a medical practice."

Many of the women are sincere when they post these ads, paid for with money borrowed from the men who pose as "marriage brokers" or "matchmakers" but whose only purpose is to exploit them.

In many cases, the matchmaker business is a front. The women exchange letters with a fake potential husband, receive money to meet that potential husband in another country, and may actually meet a man playing the part. Some Rohypnol in a drink, and the woman wakes in her new "home," a brothel, informed she has to "work off" the cost of the ticket plus interest, work off the cost of her room and board, her clothing. Those are some expensive items, because payback takes years.

The women who sign with the "legitimate" matchmaking services often end up no better.

At first, everything with the new husband in a foreign land is blissful. A few years later, after a child or two, the women find out the bargain is one-sided. Their "job" is to stay home and make babies.

Often, the husband excludes the wife from family events—she doesn't speak her husband's language, after all, and gets no encouragement to learn. The man has essentially paid for a domestic slave, one who cleans his house, cooks his meals, and, because of her upbringing, doesn't refuse his demands for sex.

If a bought-bride does protest, the result can be verbal, emotional, or physical abuse. If the wife becomes too troublesome, the husband can kick her out.

Some men have even hidden green cards or have notified the INS that the marriage has been dissolved, making the woman now an illegal alien.

For the women who manage to get a divorce, many have lost custody of their children. If that happens and if the woman gets deported, she may never be allowed to see her children again.

Then, there is the lowest of the low. Kidnappers, who see the potential largess in snatching a young, pretty girl, of any age, off the streets. The victims are immediately raped and sold to a *Mafiya* pimp. The "lucky" ones get set up in dormitories, where they are fed and get medical treatment for unwanted pregnancies or sexually transmitted infections.

They don't receive condoms, usually because the customer doesn't want to use them. In the worse-case scenario, they are denied abortions on religious grounds but receive punishment for getting pregnant. Many are kept compliant with drug addiction and the continued promise they can work their "debts" off, that they'll be freed when that happens.

But this debt compounds like interest. They will never pay it off.

They can't say no to a customer. They can't insist he wear a condom. Those not killed by drug addiction die from AIDS. (AIDS is quickly becoming the scourge of the former Soviet Union, and much like the U.S. in the 1980s, the governments pretend it doesn't exist. At the root of the rapid spread of this disease in Russia, for example, is typical Russian fatal-ism: If I die, I die.)

The twisted dependency of the *Mafiya* on police indifference, proportionate to the bribes they receive, means these whorehouses are never raided and operate at times with off-duty police providing "secu-rity." There are "games" between rival whorehouses: Women mud-wrestle each other to heavy betting. There are rumors of a house in Albania where women fight to the death. "You know," said one Russian *Mafiya* boss, "like cock fights in America, except these are cunt fights."

A woman's "career" in one of these houses ends in her late 20s, unless she can hide her age well, but the *Mafiya* boss gets a final payment from her by selling her to a colleague's porn movie studio, often ones that specialize in snuff films.

The lowest stratum of women work the streets on their own, for meager amounts of money to feed a child or to buy drugs (cut with harsh cleaning powders). Pregnancy, of course, means no income once the pregnancy begins to show. As one pimp said, "Who wants to fuck a fat pig?"

Saddest of all, women have become resigned that this is their only fate. One girl, 15 or 16, but old beyond her years, defied the orders of her pimp not to speak to me. She said, "Who would want me now as a wife? What man would marry me? I am filth. This is the only thing I can do."

And the girls in the houses and on the streets are younger and younger.

One pimp explained, "We supply what is asked for. Men want a young virgin. The trouble is you are only a virgin once, and we have to keep a constant supply or we lose customers."

The only escape the women see is death. You can't leave your house or your pimp because the punishment when you're caught is severe—and you will be caught. The *Mafiya* pay impoverished families to turn in their daughters and sisters who've escaped.

The "light" punishment is removing fingers, cuts to the face to leave disfiguring scars, further locking them into slavery.

"All cats are gray in the dark," one pimp said and laughed. "Besides, my customers are not interested in the face."

For repeated attempts to escape, the punishment is death.

The body of a 17-year-old girl from Romania was recently recovered from the Danube, her nose and breasts cut off. She had been raped so forcefully she was torn open between her vagina and anus. Police indicated she had been arrested several times for prostitution. (These numerous "arrests" are often for nothing more than walking down a street and are police extortion to get larger bribes from pimps.)

In the case of this Romanian girl, her pimp claimed the body, which he sold back to her family so they could give her a decent burial.

Yet another way a pimp gets a final payment.

When I confronted the pimp about the girl's death, he gave a customary *Mafiya* "businessman's" reply: "They're only a commodity."

Respond to Author.

CHAPTER 3

**An excerpt from *Self-Inflicted Wounds:
Dangerous Truths* (Book 2)**

The large room served as a library and office. A mishmash of book cases lined the walls, some to the ceiling, some shorter. Books, magazines, videos lined every shelf, two or three deep in some places. Several shelves bowed enough that one more item might break them and send their contents to join the chaos already occupying the worn, stained carpeting.

Small tables had been turned into desks cluttered with computers and television sets, all turned on but their volumes muted. State television played on some; CNN on others. Stacks of newspapers and magazines; dirty dishes, cups, and glasses; and overflowing ashtrays had been stacked on the floor.

Someone had cleared a space on one of the tables, and a bottle of plum brandy and three relatively clean glasses sat there.

A tall man stood by a window and smoked. He was thin, his clothes loose and haphazard, his countenance dark and rough-featured.

When Djindjic closed the door, the voices and music were muffled. He inclined his head toward the other man and looked at Mai. "Stanimir Ateljević, this is Katherine Burke," he said, using one of Mai's aliases.

Ateljević said nothing, and Djindjic went to the table with the brandy and poured four fingers into each glass. He picked up a glass and looked at Mai. She and Ateljević took their glasses at the same time.

Djindjic toasted everyone's health, "except Milošević." They drank, and the sweet, strong brandy slipped easily down the throat.

Ateljević settled a heavy-lidded, sullen gaze on Mai. "I heard you wished to speak with me. What about?"

"The murders of Milošević's friends," Mai said.

The two men exchanged a glance, not a guilty one but surprise.

"Who are you again?" Ateljević asked.

"My name is Katherine Burke. I work for the U.N."

"The U.N. or NATO?"

"The U.N."

"What do you do for the U.N.?"

"Officially, I'm in the business of refugee relief."

Ateljević drank brandy and studied her over the rim of his glass. "And unofficially?"

"I gather information."

EuroScene
Dateline: Belgrade

A Flood of Violence

FROM: Stanimir Ateljević, Speech at a Recent Protest

Citizens,

Mine is a simple message. We cannot have democracy without democratic elections.

But in a country suffering under Milošević, we cannot expect a democratic vote. We can't even hope for it.

Why?

Because of Milošević, we are about to drown in a flood of violence.

We must protest that violence loudly and demand not only a democratic election but also democratic order in our country.

We all want to live in a nonviolent country, but first we have to teach ourselves what peace means for us. But this flood of violence leaves us in perpetual survival mode, scared, helpless, and losing hope. The only cure for this is a democratic state. However, we have neither democracy nor a state.

But we can build both, and in so doing there are things we must have: Kosovo must remain a part of that democratic state so that Serbs there may live in peace there, so that Serbs who fled terror there and became refugees in their own land can return home. There can be no further break-up of the state we have. All ethnicities, who are our friends, belong here.

In the past decade, this flood of violence has inundated us like a tsunami. Its intensity seems sudden and new, but it is not. It has been a continual flood for a half century or more. Some have told us to meet that violence with more violence, that we have to revenge the wrongs done to us. We must resist that temptation. That is the easy way, but democracy comes only after the hard work. When we finally complete our work for this democratic state we cannot have revanchism*. We must cast extremism aside and assure we do not have revanchism. The only way to assure this is a democratic election.

We also desperately need national reconciliation. Serbs must, as the Americans say, bury the hatchet—

in the ground not in someone's face or back, even if this has been done to us. We must end division, stop the arbitrary separation of citizens into groups labeled "Patriots" and "Traitors." Our current rulers call themselves Patriots but of Milošević's many sins, the worst are against his own people and Serbia. That is no patriot, and the people of Serbia are not traitors for opposing him.

He must go.

Our democratic state must be different from what we have now and not only to stem the flood. The elite who rules us now does not share our desire for democracy. But recently, we see that this violence has begun to thin the herd so that the few obsolete survivors stand alone. I know many here are of Milošević's party, but you are here because you know the state as it is now will only drown in that violence, because you know Milošević has failed you and betrayed all who trusted him. Now, he can no longer trust those who were loyal to him, and no new allies are rushing to his aid. The dwindling number of his sycophants distrust each other too much to govern.

Now, another river fuels the flood of violence, one from beyond our borders. The powerful in Washington, in Brussels, with their sanctions and their bombs in support of terrorism from Kosovo intensify the flood. These power-brokers tell us they are acting from humanitarian interests. Serbs have starved under these sanctions, have had their environment poisoned, and we are supposed to believe them when they say this has been done for our benefit?

It is all violence, flooding us.

We must survive. We *must* survive.

We must stop the violence from within and not look away from that external violence from the United States and from NATO. We must never think it is for our benefit, that it is to help us. If we ever do, we have lost ourselves as Serbs.

We will never be free of the foreign violence that enslaves us until we dam our internal violence. Only we can do this. We will reject assistance from the very entities who brought violence to us from outside. Otherwise, we will simply exchange one master for another who could be worse. If we do not do this on our own, we must acknowledge our disgrace and not call ourselves Serbs.

The slavery we now endure is much more significant than petty political differences. A democratic Serbia and the fight against violence from any source are what will unite us. And we will win this war!

Once we win, we must remember our power comes only from the people. Any power we have is not absolute nor permanent. Only Serbia is unending. A free and democratic Serbia. That is what we fight for. And with God as our champion, we will create a Serbia that is free.

Thank you.

*Revanchism is a political policy of revenge or violent recovery of territory lost in war.

Respond to Author.

CHAPTER 4

An excerpt from *Self-Inflicted Wounds: Welcome to Belgrade* (Book 1)

Nelson said, *"These assassinations, which the lovesick lawyer recently accused you of, plus a litany of others in Yugoslavia are reaching a tipping point. The police, of course, are barely investigating, except in the case of Arkan's murder."*

"Only because that was so public, and he was such a hero to so many," Mai said.

Nelson nodded and continued, *"These killings have been going on for almost a decade but have increased in the past several months. The victims are major and minor government officials, journalists, military officers, police, and collateral victims caught in the overkill. The conviction rate is almost nil … State's decided it's time for a change in Yugoslavia. Change at the top."*

"I thought after the Dayton talks, this administration declared Milošević was the only person it could deal with," Mai said.

"Kosovo changed that. Pissed the President off royally. That's why we dumped several thousand tons of bombs on the country last year. State wants the Milošević regime destabilized, but it has to look as if it's from within. And they want Milošević out, also from within."

"The most efficient way to do that might be to let the murders continue."

Nelson shook his head. "That's the easy way, and what if it isn't Milošević behind it but the opposition? A replacement for him must come from the opposition, but State doesn't want someone with blood on his hands."

That would be a first, she thought.

EuroScene
Dateline: Belgrade

Blood and Tears
(Belgrade Correspondent)

It was Orthodox Easter Sunday, 1999. A beautiful day in spring. The NATO bombing was on a brief hiatus. A perfect day for couples to stroll hand in hand, and that's what this one couple did. They took a long walk. They spoke with friends. They had lunch, lingered over it, and headed home. The sun was warm, the day brilliant. A day to cast off the cares of work and to spend together.

The difference between this couple and all others enjoying the day was that this couple was constantly watched and recorded by state security, the dreaded Secret Police.

The surveillance team's report might have looked like this:

"Subjects left apartment at 1:53 p.m., walked on Knez Mihailova Street. Spoke with an old couple in front of the Russian Tsar Cafe. Talked to a bearded man who wore glasses for a quarter hour. Subjects walked in Kalemegdan Park until 3:53 p.m. Lunched at 3:56 p.m. at Kolarac Restaurant. Alone. Left restaurant at 4:27 p.m. Walked toward their residence on 48 Molerova Street. At 4:58 p.m. we received orders to cease surveillance."

Two minutes later at exactly 5:00 p.m., three men approached the couple and, without warning, shot the man point-blank with machine guns. The three fled the scene in a car and were lost in traffic.

The wife, unhurt, cradled her husband's body, her tears mixing with his blood.

Slavko Čuruvija died on the sidewalk before the entrance to his apartment building. So close to safety but so far away. Yet another friend of Milošević to be killed in the past decade.

Čuruvija was a noted journalist, a publisher of or contributor to journals censored after the passage of a 1998 law. This law allowed the authorities to shut down any publication, television programme, or radio station that "threatened national security."

In other words, any part of the media that had criticised Milošević.

Media in Belgrade speculated Milošević himself requested the law and the parliament, controlled by his party, passed it. The Serbian Parliament isn't called "Slobo's Rubber Stamp" without cause.

Čuruvija had been the first and the loudest to denounce the law and Milošević for it. He did so in publications that wouldn't censor him: *The Daily Telegraph*, the *Weekly Telegraph*, and *European Magazine*. However, he'd committed other "serious offense." For example, in his writing he didn't refer to ethnic Albanians in Kosovo as murderers or terrorists. He was the first journalist to publish a graphic of the symbol for *Otpor*, the organization of pro-democracy students, a stylized clenched fist.

This offense resulted in a heavy fine (millions of dollars) and a five-month jail sentence.

Until that law and the legal action, Čuruvija and Milošević had been close friends. Čuruvija and his wife were part of the Milošević/Markovic inner circle, among the privileged few.

A fall from the heights of power to bleeding to death on Easter Sunday in your wife's arms.

Čuruvija's wife [name withheld for her protection], who is an historian, Čuruvija's friends, and the average person on the street believe the surveillance of Čuruvija was called off deliberately, so the Secret Police would have free rein to murder him.

This cadre of secret police is sometimes called "Milošević's Hidden Hand." They are "special operations" police and are believed to have spread terror in Kosovo in 1999. Other nicknames are the "Men in Black," for the black, ninja-like garb they prefer; the Frenkies or Frenki's Boys, after their first commander, Franko Simatović. They are, simply, Milošević's secret army, who have no constraints but who have immunity from police attention.

Yugoslavia and Serbia, its largest province, have many layers of police and special operations units, equivalents of SWAT and special forces. Whatever the secret police call this unit, the consensus is they are merely trained killers. Think of them as Milošević's praetorian guard. They operate under the auspices of the government but are completely outside the law. Their purpose? Settling personal scores for Milošević and his family.

Says Čuruvija's wife, "Seeing the mechanism of an ugly state, seeing how the state security agency has been turned into the political police, is so horrifying."

Official, government spokespersons respond, somewhat foot in mouth, "Internal security only goes after the enemies of Serbia."

It all rather depends on one's perspective.

This Easter was gloomy and wet, but people remembered a journalist had died in the street.

He wasn't the first nor the last, but the average Serb shrugs. Such is life—and death—in Serbia.

Respond to Author.

CHAPTER 5

An excerpt from *Self-Inflicted Wounds:*
Welcome to Belgrade (Book 1)

Mai had lined the walls with sections of foam board. Each had photographs taped to them and hand-written notes. Alexei walked over to the closest and took it in: a picture of a man, his name neatly printed beneath the photo, as well as his position in the government and relationship to Milošević. There was personal information about dress, routine, marital status, number of children, and a chronology of movements....

Another foam board listed a number of men. No pictures, only brief bios and dates of their deaths. Mai had written, "Official reports indicate 'accidents' or 'sui-

cides.'" She'd emphasized that with a question mark and an exclamation point.

Alexei's lips lifted in a smile. Both he and Mai had taken to the computer age in espionage quite well, but she liked some things to be hands-on....

Some of the murders stretched back to the mid-nineties, but Mai had found the links among them: all had been shot and no suspects had been taken or, in some cases, even identified.

The three men she'd been accused of killing, she'd used a red marker to place an X over their faces. Next to them were more names and pictures with the label, "Potential targets." Among them was another famous name, Ivan Stambolić, Milošević's mentor, the man who'd accidentally made him who he was, though Stambolić now was another harsh critic.

The board with the picture of a man named Bosko Perošević stopped his casual perusal of the boards. Perošević was governor of Vojvodina province and headquartered in Novi Sad, some sixty miles away. In her neat, block printing, Mai had written in all capitals, in red, and underlined, "Next." Beside that was a date, two days from now.

Alexei turned away from that board and closed his eyes, his heart sinking. He told himself this wasn't evidence Mai was identifying targets. Yet, when he opened his eyes again, the evidence was all around....

Mai had always been more into saving souls than making kills, but he more than anyone knew how her cynicism had deepened in the past five years after she'd failed to stop a disillusioned soldier from the worst act of domestic terrorism the U.S. had ever seen.

He went back to the board on Perošević and jotted down the date, time, and location she written there. If Mai was going to be in Novi Sad in two days, so would he. No, he'd be there before her.

EuroScene
Dateline Belgrade

Crisis or Contrivance?
(Belgrade Correspondent)

AMONG THE VICTIMS are an indicted war criminal, a provincial governor, the head of Yugoslav Aviation, former paramilitary commanders, magistrates, journalists, and several innocent bystanders. Except for the innocent bystanders, the common thread among all these murder victims is their association with Slobodan Milošević.

Before their murders or "suicides," the dead had fallen out of favor with Milošević or had voiced disagreement with a government position or policy. None of them were affiliated with any organized opposition party, but most of them were, at some point, close enough to Milošević to make their murders a hot topic in Belgrade.

Of course, you have to be careful what you say. If your voice is a bit too loud and your sentiment is that Milošević is ridding himself of people who knew too much or who had slighted him in some way, you might find yourself approached by young men, who materialize from a crowd at the market or the clientele at a cafe.

If you're lucky, you might only feel the force of their fists and boots. If you're not lucky, they might be secret police or people in the hire of the secret police, and their vindication of the reputation of the Balkan strongman could be deadly for you.

The government line—i.e., Milošević's line—is these murders, which have accumulated over a decade, have been committed by either "agents of NATO" or "the CIA" at the direction of the American president and/or the British prime minister.

Police—which have so many overlapping jurisdictions—collect evidence to a certain extent. Not to do so would appear unseemly to the public, but arrests and trials are rare.

The notorious paramilitary commander Arkan, who blamed CNN for his indictment by the War Crimes Tribunal, was murdered in public in the Intercontinental Hotel in January. Indeed, his murder was the one that drew the west's attention to the long line of victims. Suspects are in custody, but no trial has been scheduled. A key suspect, not yet arrested, recently died at the end of a car chase Belgraders can't stop talking about.

The western media point to Arkan's murder as the first, but the reality is that local officials, provincial officials, judges, police officers have been dropping like flies for more than a decade. Again, the person who connects all their deaths is Milošević. Because of this, despite strong circumstantial evidence, police look the other way.

Europe looks upon this as a looming crisis. None of the murders have extended beyond the borders of the disintegrating Yugoslavia, but the fear is that will change. Moreover, the number of murders and the individuals targeted are reaching a tipping point where the whole bureaucratic hierarchy could be neutered. If the winter of 1999-2000 was bad, the next one with no functionaries to assure even illegal fuel is obtained and distributed could be catastrophic. Belgrade might be reduced to the dire straights of

Sarajevo in the early 1990s, where every tree, bush, and stick of wood in the city was used for fuel, followed by private book collections from homes, libraries, and universities. (Belgrade University's head librarian has vowed to protect his books with his life.) It could be that bad, and everyone knows it. However, they don't voice it, not with roving bands of thugs dispensing their form of justice.

The government declares these murders have nothing that distinguishes them from common crimes. If not blamed on NATO or the CIA, Albanian "terrorists" or gypsies get the blame. The government's information minister has said, "What crisis? Only the west calls it a crisis. They would love for it to be one, because it is they who conspire to subjugate the Serb people."

Others say Milošević, though burdened with a history of depression and being the son of two suicides, is a crafty statesman. He is too smart, they say, to be behind the murders of his friends and associates. Perhaps.

Or is it someone close to Milošević who seeks to serve him in that way faithful courtiers did after over-hearing a drunken Henry II mutter about Thomas a Beckett.

"Who will rid me of this troublesome priest?"

There has been no blood in the cathedrals of Belgrade. Yet. There has been plenty in the streets, and Serbs await the next murder, some with trepidation; some with anticipation.

Respond to Author.

CHAPTER 6

An excerpt from *Self-Inflicted Wounds: Welcome to Belgrade* (Book 1)

Mai had wanted more flexibility in her lodging than the hotels most journalists used. Under one of her ubiquitous cover names, she rented a modest house near the city center. The owner had overcome the narrowness of the lot by building the boxy, concrete and brick house with three levels. However, its hints of disuse in the faded exterior whitewash and worn interior furnishings fit her cover as a freelance journalist.

Besides, she knew quite well journalists' hotel rooms got searched by the police on a regular basis. Not much of an issue for a real journalist but a big one for a spy whose cover was being a journalist.

Her cover wasn't for show. She joined the media in covering the nightly demonstrations and bought her colleagues plenty of drinks in the hotels' bars. They discussed the murders, yes, but the big story was the daily and nightly protests on the streets of Belgrade.

*The large, organized marches with their slogan-chanting were the brainchildren of an opposition group composed mostly of university students—*Otpor, *the Serbian word for resistance. The* Otpor-*run protests didn't have the same spontaneity as the ones during the NATO bombings, when housewives, doctors, waitresses, and even some government workers took to the streets wearing paper targets in defiance of NATO and Miloše-vić.* Otpor *had built on that success and enhanced it, given the number of arrests each day. However, because of the media presence, the reaction of Milošević's police had been unusually understated.*

Another topic of discussion among the freelancers was the large number of them, especially in a regime notori-ously uncooperative with a free press. Each had a story of lining the pocket of some Milošević toady with the exor-bitant "licensing fees" they'd paid. Further speculation addressed the likelihood the government was laying off the demonstrators in the hope they'd be seen in a negative light, that it would seem like Milošević was simply a beleaguered head of state trying to assure public safety.

However, the reporters did what they always did—romanticized it.

Mai often strayed from the police-designated press areas to take pictures and conduct interviews. Her smile and her good Serbian got people to open up, but as she snapped photos of the protests, she also took pictures of government leaders going about their business in the background. How fortunate for her the demonstrators preferred government buildings as their backdrop.

After joining reporters for drinks, and turning down the occasional invitation for private drinks in someone's hotel room, she would return to the unassuming house, download her pictures, and compose her EuroScene blog. She would nap before slipping from the house and flouting the curfew to shadow opposition leaders to and from their clandestine meetings.

Undetected, Alexei had watched her….

EuroScene
Dateline: Belgrade

An Evening in Belgrade
(Belgrade Correspondent)

THE CROWD before the Yugoslav Parliament Building has an air of a street party, as if neighbors had emerged from their homes after work to enjoy a pleasant, spring evening. Rock music blares from dozens of radios, all tuned to B2-92, Belgrade's non-government radio station. The crowd sings along to the music. Couples dance, some while holding their signs over head. The signs read, "Slobo must go!" The crowd periodically takes up that chant.

Vendors from the various open-air markets have picked up and moved to where the crowd gathers. There is good business in selling bottles of water and ice cream bars.

For a city that experienced its share of deprivation and power outages during the winter, this steamy night is a treat. Summer is on its way, and everything looks brighter, better.

The only shadow on the party-like atmosphere is the presence of the watchful police, determined to suppress any protest of the continued rule of Serbian strongman, Slobodan Milošević.

One protester isn't afraid to give his name. David Mladinovic says, "We are like protesters in America in 1960s. Hell no! He must go!"

The wording of a demonstrator gone home long before Mladinovic was born might be slightly off, but the sentiment is the same.

The protestors are mostly young, mainly university students, members of the student resistance group *Otpor*. But among them are older men and women, hovering at the edge of the crowd. They share the sentiments of the younger protesters, but the dancing is a bit too wild for them. They want to be a part of this, but they aren't sure how to go about it.

And with age and experience comes the fear the young do not have.

The police, after all, are decked out in riot gear. Mostly, the police congregate on the opposite end of the plaza from the protesters, and they have fire trucks with water cannons standing by.

Even if the police do not act, there are the surveillance cameras, and people of every age know the police will scour the tapes and identify as many protestors as possible. The older people are more afraid of that middle-of-the-night battering down of the front door than the young ones, who as yet have no job to lose or children to protect.

The crowd grows in the center of the plaza at the foot of the steps of the parliament building. Milošević's Parliament they call it. In Milošević's regime, the true and free election of members of that body is always under question. Rumors are rife about unopened ballot boxes from areas hostile to Milošević ending up in the Danube or the Sava.

The crowd ends up between us in the media and the police. None of the media is from state radio or television. CNN and other major American networks are there, as is the BBC and a few French networks, but none of the name reporters, only local stringers. Unless, of course, things heat up, like, for example, if the police start shooting instead of beating. Then, the big names will show up, provided they're willing to pay the bribe demanded by a minor Interior Ministry functionary to get work permits.

We freelancers, hungry for the career-making story, pay the bribes without question, and we hand government censors one story while we file another.

It's about 10 p.m. local time now, and the "party" starts to break up. Until some men wade into the crowd, chanting "Slobo must go!" with their fists raised. They wear black and white *keffiyehs*, wrapped to hide their faces. The crowd takes up the chant and the fist waving with them, and the music from the radios is drowned out.

These can't be true protestors. They're too organized. They moved through the crowd with a purpose and a plan. They're too burly and bulked up to be university students. They're police or soldiers, sent in by the police to stir up the crowd and give the police an excuse to use the water cannons or tear gas or batons or rubber bullets.

Yugoslavia is in the midst of a series of unsolved murders of government officials and prominent figures, but the police are too busy quelling nonviolent protests to solve crimes. Priorities, like most everything else about this regime, are skewed.

Now, one of the masked men throws bricks at the police, and where did he find them, you may ask. Why, indeed? The plaza isn't large, and the police are a stone's throw away, literally, and the brick isn't a brick but a piece of one, a piece small enough to be concealed within a winter jacket worn out of season.

The tear gas comes in response, three or four shots to disperse the crowd, which melts away into side streets and alleys, leaving the masked men behind, men whom the police leave untouched.

That leaves the media. Our backs are up against the wall of a nearby government building, and most of us don't know Belgrade well enough to risk retreating via alleys and back streets. Cameras still clicking or whirring away, some of us shift, trying to out-flank the approaching police. Riot shields up, they form into a phalanx and charge as a single, sinuous snake.

We break and run, and the phalanx disintegrates, two or three police breaking off to run down a reporter. The batons start to swing, but most of us get away unscathed. Later, at the bar at the Intercontinental, we discover no one got arrested, but some of us have new battle scars. A French reporter needs stitches, at least 12 of them. An Italian reporter gets his cracked ribs bound by a cameraman who used to be a military medic. The rest of us sport bruises, a broken nose or finger, none the worse for the wear. As the booze flows, we become more talkative.

A Dutch photographer sums the evening up.

"The people of Belgrade will sleep well tonight. We kept the nightsticks off their backs."

Respond to Author.

CHAPTER 7

An excerpt from *Self-Inflicted Wounds:*
***Dangerous Truths* (Book 2)**

Mai left the car and walked up crumbling concrete stairs to a house needing a coat of paint or several. The etched glass double doors bespoke a previous gentility, but for a clandestine rendezvous, it served its purpose. She knocked, and an indistinct form appeared behind the frosted glass. One door opened, allowing the scent of sweaty bodies and stale cigarette smoke to escape. A TV-handsome man, salt and pepper hair, stood in the opening. After a few seconds he remembered his security protocols and stepped aside. His bright eyes regarded her with skepticism.

"It's been a while," said Zoran Djindjic.

"Yes, it has. Did he come?"

"It took some convincing, but he's here. Come in."

Mai went in, closing the door behind her. She tugged her gloves off and pushed her sunglasses up on her head. To her left was a dining room with four men around the table holding a phone, a laptop, a printer, and reams of paper. Young men debated the contents of a flyer they designed. Music screamed from somewhere in the house. B2-92, the Belgrade rock station the government had tried to shut down.

In one corner of the dining room, open boxes held white tee-shirts emblazoned with the Otpor *stylized fist. Stacks of bumper stickers with the same logo were scattered about on every surface.*

The room was thick with cigarette smoke, perhaps some of it marijuana, and the table was littered with the detritus of their meals and empty brandy bottles. The men gave her a desultory look before they went back to smoking and arguing above the volume of the music.

☙ ☙

EuroScene
Dateline: Belgrade

Heroes or Hooligans?
(Belgrade Correspondent)

THAT DEPENDS on your point of view. Since the NATO War (a Serbian term), neither western governments nor NATO itself have been the instigator of change in the former Yugoslavia. That distinction falls to the public in the form of what started out in the mid-1990s as student protests for the removal of professors who'd questioned the Milošević regime.

Otpor—literally, "resistance"—is one example of a grassroots movement, which has grown to be the most significant and visual form of disgust with the government in Yugoslavia. *Otpor* is the action arm, purveyors of graffiti, bumper stickers, T-shirts, rock concerts, and pithy anti-regime chants at the staged, pro-Milošević rallies.

If *Otpor* is action, the independent radio station B2-92 is the voice of the resistance. Originally B92, it broadcast on 92.5 MHz. The government brought it into the state media fold, but some of the original founders set up programming again as B2-92. Now, B2-92 uses music to define a movement and to explain the conditions of life in Belgrade. Loud and raucous rock music suits this perfectly. As a listener said of B2-92's programming, "It was as if the expression in that painting 'The Scream' received a voice."

Both *Otpor* and B2-92 give voice to Belgraders' frustrations, a long not-so-silent scream that says, "We have had enough!"

Otpor is everywhere. Not in terms of members, but in symbology. In a brilliant usage of the corporate concept of branding, *Otpor* has summed up its philosophy in a single graphic: the upraised, clenched fist. That logo is everywhere, much to the dismay of the regime. As fast as police rip down the posters and unpeel the stickers or arrest people wearing the T-shirts or ticket their cars for sporting a bumper sticker, replacements appear. One can almost envision a group of *Otpor* members lurking around the corner, waiting for the police to leave before they dash from cover and slap posters back on the walls.

The black-and-white fist is everywhere.

Nor can the police quell B2-92's voice. When the secret police shut it down, the broadcasters pack up their transmitters and move to another location. If their equipment gets confiscated, they borrow more. Or they send tapes of their broadcasts to Romania or some other nearby country for them to be broadcast and picked up Belgrade. When the regime jams their signal, they un-jam it or jam state media broadcasts.

Milošević's fear of *Otpor* and B2-92 borders on pathological. He commands state media to accuse them both of illegal activities (congregating without the appropriate permits or broadcasting without the required licenses). Or that they take money from the west marked for the overthrow of the government.

(*Otpor* and B2-92 have taken money from western aid organizations, including USAID and the European Union, strictly, they say, for survival purposes. The amount of money is certainly not enough to overthrow an entrenched government.)

The head of B2-92 has managed to evade arrest by taking frequent "holidays" in Montenegro. However, thousands of *Otpor* members have been taken into custody, mostly for the "offense" of wearing an *Otpor* T-shirt or putting a clenched-fist decal on the windscreen of a car.

However, *Otpor* has no real leader. It keeps no roster of members, but it has grown beyond the status of a "student movement." People from all walks of life identify themselves as members. The unknown group determining its actions understand that having no definite hierarchy is to their benefit. If *Otpor* is "organized" into cells, no one cell knows the plans of the other cells.

"That way," said one veteran *Otpor* agitator, "if the police take some of us, we don't give away anyone else. The police here, they can get you to talk."

Most of the time, when the police crack down on either *Otpor* or B2-92, it backfires on the regime. Rather than discouraging people from joining *Otpor* or listening to B2-92, the harsh treatment only swells the ranks and increases the audience.

The police have used their traditional methods to break *Otpor*—infiltration, bribes, threats to families, the usual tactics of a scared, teetering regime. But such tactics didn't drive members away. It made people more resolved toward change. "Don't tell me where you're from," is quite often the greeting at rallies. That way, they won't implicate anyone else when the police come to "chat."

Instead of avoiding repression, *Otpor* members welcome it. Each arrest, each beating brings more people to the resistance. Each time B2-92 is shut down, it resumes with more listeners.

However, the regime and its secret police see in *Otpor* the potential for urban guerrillas in a war for people's hearts and minds, a war that the regime will pull out all stops to win. But *Otpor's* clenched fist assaults the eyes of the government. B2-92 is the mouthpiece that screams "Resistance!" to anyone who can tune a radio. The regime wants silence, but neither *Otpor* nor B2-92 will shut up. To the regime, that is unacceptable: "We've told you to be quiet, and you won't. Who do you think you are?"

They consider themselves people with a united voice screaming against the wilderness of a regime stretched to its breaking point.

Respond to Author.

CHAPTER 8

An excerpt from *Self-Inflicted Wounds: Dangerous Truths* (Book 2)

Ateljević filled his and Mai's glasses with brandy. "You have something to say to me you don't want Zoran to hear," he said. "That much is obvious. What is also obvious is you'd rather be saying it to him."

"If word of what I'm about to discuss with you leaks, the offer I'll be making will be withdrawn, and who knows who might find out you spoke with an 'agent of the west,'" Mai said.

Ateljević smiled for the first time, smug and confident. "I doubt that."

"Don't ever doubt my convictions."

"All right. What's the offer?"

"The U.S. State Department have picked you as the person they are most willing to work with in a Yugoslavia without Milošević."

Ateljević barked with laughter. "This would be the administration who has said Milošević is the only hope for peace in the Balkans?"

"Those are the public sentiments. Privately, they understand the reality of what another decade of Milošević means to peace and stability in Europe."

"Is this supposed to make me happy?" Ateljević asked, an edge to his voice. "U.S. aircraft bombed my country last year. Pardon me if I don't jump for joy at an offer to set me up in power."

"No, not set you up. You'll have to be elected as legitimately as possible in this country. There will be some monetary support for your campaign and a willingness to deal once you're in office."

"CIA protection for me while I run for office?"

"No."

"I didn't think so. You Americans like to lob bombs but not shed your own blood."

"I'm not an American. Here's what they'll give you. Campaign contributions, as I said, attention in the world press that the U.S. and NATO would approve of your presidency, a distinct possibility of lifting sanctions, and, once you're elected, investment capital in exchange for certain nation-building actions."

He raised his glass and again regarded her over its rim. "Why didn't the State Department send someone to talk to me?"

Bloody hell, Mai thought, who the fuck do you think I am? "Plausible deniability," she said.

"In case I lose?"

"In case you say no."

EuroScene
Dateline: Belgrade

Reality
A Speech by Stanimir Ateljević

I HAVE to speak to you at this rally using a bullhorn because everything that should be the voice of the people—the independent media—has been gagged. This rally is happening even though it is not allowed, and so this rally becomes the voice of those who have been tortured, beaten, imprisoned. Such things will not silence us, will not numb us. Instead, we feel each blow on our brothers and sisters as if it were on us.

In Serbia, thinking is dangerous to an unthinking regime. This is why they have closed our universities. For the few universities still open, the police are present when students take examinations to assure no one exchanges ideas. The regime has made certain that those who desire an education cannot get it. The universities have no autonomy and are made to propagate rules for students that are more fitting for jails.

Why does this happen? A Serbian poet gives us the answer: Knowledge is power. Knowledge is power. This regime has decided it is the only one who can wield power, so because it fears knowledge, it must destroy knowledge.

Knowledge is power. When we saw the evil inflicted on us by NATO, that knowledge became our power. That power leads us to repair that damage, to rebuild. In that way, we were victorious against NATO because they did not defeat our knowledge. Restoration has come from our power, our knowledge, the knowledge of our engineers and workers, not from the regime's empty slogans.

Knowledge makes us thirst for more, enhancing our power. In response, from its fear of knowledge, the regime offers a new anti-terrorism law. But they have set the bar so low that any citizen can be considered a terrorist. Today the regime calls us traitors. Tomorrow it will declare us terrorists.

Instead of focusing these anti-terrorism laws against the KLA [Kosovo Liberation Army], these laws focus on us. To the regime, the voice of the people, the power we have from our knowledge makes us terrorists. Now, terrorism is legal for the real terrorists.

This must not happen. Every day we must oppose this regime in large ways and small; oppose it with nonviolence, with knowledge and power, but most of all with truth. The rallies must spread throughout Serbia and must include all parties, all individuals. Everyone must deny this regime—judges, university presidents, all faculty, all students.

We must say no to this regime's violence and its deceiving us, loudly and constantly until those in power understand that their violence and lies are not only senseless but hopeless. Together, we must isolate those in power, make them stand alone. They must learn from our knowledge, our power, that the only way out is democratic elections.

Milošević must go, but by elections that do not leave a gaping hole for an outsider to fill. Only a Serb can protect Serbs. For this election result, all opposition parties must unite. Yes, we have our differences, but, like knowledge, that is our strength. Once we have succeeded in the elections, we can have civil debate and do so without concern because we will be what we are not now—a democracy.

Leading up to the elections, working together means not only the parties but also trade unions, student groups, scientific organizations, and artist guilds. There can be no contention among us. We must unite so together we can rise. That is the only platform we need.

Thank you.

Respond to Author.

CHAPTER 9

An excerpt from *Self-Inflicted Wounds: Dangerous Truths* (Book 2)

*T*he murders are a part of Milošević's convoluted plan to make him president for life," said Ateljević. "He's good at making opportunities, but he does nothing unless it's completely thought out, with all the implications and permutations addressed. He makes opportunities, which look like happenstance."

"He's a politician," Mai said, shrugging.

"One who is eliminating any possible rivals to his power and getting revenge for any slights, real or perceived. He's behind this all right, but I think you've figured that out. However, you have to prove it. If it's him, he's put plenty of layers between him and the 'hired help' and has spread plenty of money around to keep people quiet."

"Why is the obvious question," Mai said.

Djindjic held up a sheaf of papers. "Have you seen this?" he asked her.

Mai took the document and skimmed the first page. It bore a government seal, and the language had a certain bureaucratic formality. "I speak decent Serbian, but my command of reading the language doesn't extend beyond a newspaper."

"That's a copy of a bill presented by Milošević's party in parliament," Djindjic explained. "It amends the Constitution to allow the president four consecutive terms, expands the circumstances wherein the president can declare martial law, and rescinds Montenegro's semi-autonomous status."

"Don't forget the president can now be elected by a simple majority of the voters, no matter the size of the turnout," Ateljević said.

"Milošević's current, second term expires next July," Mai said. "A shrewd move on the face of it, given the fact the two of you who lead the largest opposition parties have vowed to boycott the elections. Faced with loss of autonomy, Montenegro will declare its independence, and we'll have yet another Balkan war."

As Mai handed the document back to Djindjic, she saw Ateljević's eye roll in her periphery.

"Have no doubt he'll use the murders to his advantage," Djindjic said. *"To crack down further on the press, move troops into the city. And if the police were to, all of a sudden, discover the perpetrators, Milošević will spin it to show he has assured the safety of the people."*

Mai said, *"I envision a big shoot-out, killing all the assassins. The police get medals, and Milošević declares how his regime has thwarted agents of the west."*

"The legislation will pass, but it will have been enough of a crisis he can call for early elections."

"So, U.N. information-gatherer," Ateljević began, *"you need to find the assassins first and get them to talk, to implicate Milošević or someone close to him. Do that, and I'll consider not boycotting the elections."*

EuroScene
Dateline: Belgrade

A Constitution is Only Paper
(Belgrade Correspondent)

IN A MOVE TODAY hailed by Serbian Nationalists as heroic and by opposition leaders as cowardly, the Federal Parliament in Belgrade unanimously passed a Constitutional amendment permitting four consecutive terms for the president. The dizzying speed at which the amendment passed took no one by surprise. Yugoslavia didn't invent the term "rubber stamp," but its parliament epitomizes it.

Milošević promptly called for a presidential election one year early and announced his candidacy.

Barring a miracle, it seems Milošević will be president of both Serbia and Yugoslavia for another eight, long years.

As fits his style, Milošević didn't enter into any discussions about the amendment, and there was no debate of its merits. With his typical manufactured humility, Milošević, after the vote, declared the results as a vote of confidence—for him.

However, discontent with Milošević has increased since the NATO bombing of last year, even though he appears to be fully entrenched in power. No member of the opposition has stepped forward to challenge him, though rumors are that former President Ivan Stambolić is considering a run.

The various police forces—regular and para-police —the secret police, and the army are all still behind Milošević.

And given the recent string of murders and disappearances of government officials who might oppose Milošević, no one seems to be willing to commit fully to running against him.

A prominent opposition leader, who requested his name be withheld, said, "Even if someone were to run, someone the people want, like Stambolić, do you really think Milošević will acknowledge that anyone except him has won? If you dredge the Danube or the Sava after election day, you might be surprised and how many ballot boxes you find. A lot of ballot boxes went missing after the last election."

Milošević's stalwart allies in parliament also seemed to have planned for any contingency. If the opposition groups do not coalescent into a single group and front a single candidate, if a dozen or more opposition leaders decide to run against him, parliament has changed the rules: The president may now be elected by a simple majority, i.e., he who has the most votes wins. For example, if a dozen opposition candidates together amass 60% of the vote and Milošević gets 40%, Milošević wins because he has more votes than any other single candidate.

This is a likely scenario, since opposition groups are further apart than ever and are divided over petty issues. Getting them to come together and support a single candidate against Milošević may be an impossibility. If that happens, they have sealed the fate of all the people of Yugoslavia.

Respond to Author.

CHAPTER 10

An excerpt from *Self-Inflicted Wounds:*
Dangerous Truths (Book 2)

With the same disaffected sigh he'd had for his worthless morning newspaper, Ranovesić cast aside the memo from Minister Bogdanović's office. Clever wording, reminding all secretariat commanders they worked for him, and that he worked for the federal government, and therefore, etc., etc. Any police actions contrary to government policies could mean a loss of pay or pension. Or life, Ranovesić added in his head.

Why didn't Bogdanović come out and say it straight? Stop investigating who is killing Milošević's friends since he's behind it. Start cracking down on the nightly demonstrations. Implied was "if the Belgrade police don't do their jobs, the army and special units will."

Ranovesić checked his watch, stood, and pulled on his uniform coat. In the hallway, eyes focused on the exit, he brushed past members of his staff.

"Where are you off to, Boss?" one asked.

"For decent coffee," he snapped, his frown telling everyone not to invite themselves along.

He didn't stop frowning until he entered the cafe. Mai Fisher sat sipping tea, a small, red rosebud pinned to the right lapel of her jacket. Ranovesić got a coffee and a sweet and joined her.

"I guess you recognized me," she said. "Flower in the lapel works every time."

"Notice I'm not laughing. How is Bukharin?"

"Improving, though not as quickly as either of us would like. Voya, I have some information..." She trailed off when he held up a hand.

"Before you start, I have something to tell you."

She smiled, though it was more a smirk. "Go ahead."

"This morning, I and every other secretariat commander got a memo from the Serbian Interior Ministry. We can no longer work at cross purposes to the federal government. Unless I wish to lose my meager pension, I must remember that."

Her voice low, Mai asked, "Was it specifically referring to the murder investigations?"

"Of course not, but I've learned to read between the lines of official memos."

EuroScene
Dateline: Belgrade

Building a Nation
(Belgrade Correspondent)

WITH A SHRUG, Vedran Mihailović answers, "Kill me?" his own question: "What's the worst they can do to me?"

Mihailović knows the risks of being a member of the opposition, of wearing an *Otpor* T-shirt. His friends have been jailed and tortured for knowing him, his family harassed for his "treason." He has lost jobs because of it.

Like most opposition activists, Mihailović has been subject to violence his whole life and expects it. Violence is an everyday occurrence, and, as Mihailović says, "It is pointless, even selfish, to worry about it, not when we have a nation to create."

In Yugoslavia, the state-controlled media is adept at transforming the victims of violence, especially if they are members of any opposition party, into the culprits, the cause of the violence. Mihailović is one such "terrorist."

He recounts a time when he and some friends sat in a cafe talking about what most Serbian youth complain about: no jobs, no amenities. Several other young men, likely members of the State Security Service or a paramilitary police unit, interrupted them and immediately started beating them.

The regular police arrived and arrested not the black-clad bullies but Mihailović and his friends, charging them with attempted murder. Of their assailants. Mihailović and his friends spent several months in jail before being released to "await trial." One friend came close to dying in jail because his injuries from the daily beatings weren't treated.

"This is Serbia today," Mihailović says.

Mihailović is a twenty-something, a handsome hooligan, and a member of the Serbian Renewal Movement, headed by Zoran Djindjic and one of many groups with the broad goal of improving life in Serbia. He listens to B2-92. He distributes *Otpor* flyers and paraphernalia. He's never without a can of spray paint that he uses to create opposition-themed graffiti. He thinks for himself and doesn't echo the regime's official line, a dangerous tendency. He does this, he says, to have something none of his comrades has ever known—a normal life, even if they have no idea what normal is.

"What we have now is not a normal," Mihailović says. "This Milošević regime is hell on earth."

Mihailović is typical of a generation of opposition youth. Born when Tito was in power and when there was a single country named Yugoslavia, he has suffered in the politically formative years of his life under Milošević. Because he has pushed back, Mihailović is a marked man, designated a traitor and a threat to the security of the nation.

Quite the burden for such a young man, but what was his specific act of treason?

"I was working a good job," he said, "but I refused to pack lunches for a pro-Milošević rally, a rally where the government forced everyone in my company to attend. I wanted no part of it and tried to get my fellow workers to do the same. Those were the things that got me fired, got me put on an official list of 'terrorists.'"

That action was also deemed seditious, as was passing out opposition pamphlets in Milošević's home town, painting graffiti, etc. Spray-painting, if he should be caught, means a brief stint in jail. For the "crime" of handing out opposition literature, the punishment is a severe thrashing, administered on the spot.

Mihailović says, "They think beating us will weaken us and we'll give up, but they forget that a beaten dog has one final bite left in him."

Initially, the general populace disdained such mild acts of disobedience and the petty vandalism. But the people also knew they couldn't even seem to support any aspect of the opposition. If you did, the thugs would start in on you. Consequently, people like Mihailović operated like lone wolves, separate from an established opposition group so if they were captured they couldn't betray any compatriots. But as the regime designated any free thought as a crime, the opposition grew, and Mihailović and his ilk became folk heroes.

"Yeah, before prison," explains Mihailović, "I was alone. People, even my own family, were afraid to condone my actions. When I came out of prison, something was different. Strangers on the street would tell me to keep it up. They would whisper encouragement to me. To my shock, they began to intercede when the beatings started. That tells me the other side is now afraid. Of me. Of the people."

Isn't he afraid of the consequences to himself, I ask him.

"They'll only arrest me again. So what?" A shrug. "When they did that before, and it only strengthened my beliefs. Yes, they could kill me, but I believe in

God. Death doesn't scare me. Besides if they did kill me, there are hundreds to replace me."

Whether this is bravery or bluster in the face of the massive state machinery of what passes for justice in Yugoslavia remains to be seen. Still, Mihailović is followed wherever he goes, and the threats against him are constant, so constant he has become accustomed to them.

Why does he continue in the face of this?

"The people in power destroyed Serbia, and every day it gets worse," he replies. "I wake people up, show them they must fight."

However, though Mihailović is aware not everyone is as committed to personal sacrifice as he is, he forges ahead. Even though he can't get a job and the regime has spread rumors he is insane. One local official declared Mihailović a homosexual, and Serbia has no tolerance for that.

So, why not stay quiet?

"Staying quiet is a coward's way. I'm no coward," he says.

With the status of being a folk hero comes responsibility. He sticks to nonviolence, organizing rallies, spray-painting opposition slogans, and handing out flyers and tee-shirts.

His life's goal is to stage an opposition rally in Milošević's home village.

He does relish his celebrity. He accepts speaking engagements at opposition meetings, and the organized opposition movements see that he gets legal aid. Opposition leaders call him regularly to offer advice and luck.

Mihailović knows the dangers involved in speaking out, in being so overt in his opposition.

"The time has come for sacrifice, for Serbs to sacrifice for Serbia, and I will sacrifice, if need be and even if I might not see my beloved Serbia rise again," he says.

"If they kill me, my comrades will only become more committed to opposition. So, let them kill me." He shrugs yet again. "There are worse things they can do to me."

Respond to Author.

CHAPTER 11

**An excerpt from *Self-Inflicted Wounds:
Dangerous Truths* (Book 2)**

P lease, for God's sake, don't call me Madame
Secretary here. I'm Georgie. Now, you've been
in Belgrade since April, May?"

"Late April."

"Nelson's kept me advised on the mission progress, of
course, but what's your take?"

"Like most things in the Balkans. A dozen different
leads all tangled together. Corrupt police, a government
unconcerned about solving the murders."

Bancroft refilled their tea cups. "You've made the
overture to Ateljević, I understand."

"Yes. He's interested, but he didn't appreciate that a
spy brought him the offer."

Bancroft rolled her eyes. "And they say women are divas. What does he want? Me to bring it to him on a velvet pillow?"

Mai laughed at the image that invoked. "No. An undersecretary, at least, and he's concerned about protection for himself and his family. However, with Ateljević as a declared candidate, Milošević wouldn't dare touch him. It would be too obvious who'd ordered the hit, and that way Milošević can't present the election to the world as fair and legal...."

"Do you think Ateljević could revive ethnic cleansing?" Bancroft asked.

"...He's never used the term in any of his speeches and writings, but his ardent nationalism is quite apparent. He never denounced the practice and does so now by couching it as 'internal violence.' One thing he did tell me. If he becomes president and Serbs are abused anywhere in Yugoslavia, he'll take care of it."

EuroScene
Dateline: Belgrade

Opposition Boycott Ends
(Belgrade Correspondent)

THE SERBIAN RENEWAL MOVEMENT ended its planned boycott of the moved-up presidential elections. Elections were scheduled for 2001, but after passage of a constitutional amendment allowing a general election for president (before this the president was selected by parliament) and a simple majority to win, Milošević moved up the election. (His coalition still controls the parliament, and parliamentary elections were not moved up.)

The bigger news is that Stanimir Ateljević of the Serbian Democratic Party will run against Milošević for president. The Serbian Democratic party is a coalition of 15 opposition groups that often opposed each other. Whereas the SRM will not boycott, it has not yet thrown its support behind Ateljević.

Ateljević had been the most vocal supporter of the boycott of the moved-up elections until recently. When asked what changed his mind, Ateljević said, "The people can be very persuasive, and the time is right. I have talked and talked about the problems in Serbia. I decided to be part of the solution."

A U.S. State Department spokesperson committed on news of Ateljević's candidacy: "We are pleased there will be a definite choice for the people of Yugoslavia during their elections. That is what democracy is all about."

Further, the consolidation of so many opposition groups into a single force appears initially to be a formidable opponent for Milošević. Not so, says a Brussels international think tank. Milošević's ability to control the press and his shut-down of media outlets he can't control will prove too powerful for the coalition to overcome, they say.

"Independent media who don't regurgitate the regime's official line don't exist in Serbia, not when Serbian journalists get arrested for terrorism. The opposition coalition has no official voice and will never get time on State television," said the think tank spokesperson.

Even members of that opposition coalition have stated they understand the election will not be fair, but they emphasize for the first time, Milošević has a credible opponent, even if that opponent is shut away from media coverage.

How might Milošević deal with this "credible" opponent campaigning against him?

The band of street thugs who harass every opposition rally have stepped up their violence. The assassinations of government officials and suspected opposition members continue—and play into the regime's hands, who blames them on NATO, acting on behalf of the opposition. Even Ateljević uses the series of murders to his advantage in his campaigning, though he is careful not to voice support for NATO. Everyone knows he is no fan of NATO or the two most powerful western governments in NATO: the U.S. and the United Kingdom.

However, the nightly peaceful street protests grow larger and larger, and their support for Ateljević grows proportionally. Many times they now outnumber the police, who, beneath their riot gear, have hearts as Serbian as the opposition. They are beginning to look the other way.

This is a Yugoslavia (and a Serbia) different from the one Milošević could so easily manipulate a decade ago. After debilitating ethnic wars, economic disaster, and the shunning of Yugoslavia by the west, people may be united by something other than belief in their ethnic superiority.

The first chink in Milošević's armor may have appeared. After Ateljević's announcement, hundreds of posters appeared all over Belgrade: Milošević's official portrait, but the caption reads, "He is finished."

The people are tired of being fucked with.

One regular demonstrator, whose name I am withholding so there will be no reprisal, looks forward to the presidential contest. He supports Ateljević but still believes Milošević will win. He hopes, however, this election will give Milošević pause to consider this: "We are no longer the backwards child he can play with or bully to death."

Respond to Author.

An excerpt from *Self-Inflicted Wounds:*
Dangerous Truths (Book 2)

For three days, Mai had watched Ivan Stambolić jog through his neighborhood and around the sports center track between 0900 and 1100 hundred each morning, with no variation. That made it too easy for anyone who wanted to harm him. Good thing she was only shooting with The Directorate's version of the miniature Minox camera. Once Stambolić was back inside she went home and downloaded the photos for her and Alexei to study.

Most of the photos were of Stambolić, pasty white arms and legs pumping, his gym shorts and tee shirt wet with sweat; the kind of runner, Alexei remarked, "who *when you hear he's dropped dead of a heart attack while running, you aren't surprised."*

She had pictures, too, of five men who'd also watched Stambolić's methodical outings. Alexei recognized Anatole and Vladimir from his visits to White Nights. Absent from the photos were Kolya, Sasha, and Cassandra Brown. When Stambolić finished his jog and entered his apartment building, the men would scatter in two different cars, in different directions, before Mai could follow.

"I'm sorry," Alexei said. "If I were up to it, I could have followed at least one of them."

Mai chided herself for criticizing him, if only in her thoughts. She and Galena had been the ones to urge him to rest to hasten his physical recovery. Alexei hadn't protested much, and Mai suspected that was more from his dislike of mundane surveillance than fatigue.

EuroScene
Dateline: Belgrade

Where is Ivan Stambolić?
Part 1
(Belgrade Correspondent)

YESTERDAY, former Serbian President Ivan Stambolić was kidnapped in broad daylight during his daily jog, a habit so routine it set him up for his abductors.

Who kidnapped him? No one knows. No one has boasted about it. No one has asked for ransom. There is plenty of speculation, and fingers are pointed; but no one is looking for Stambolić. The Belgrade police have not confirmed the kidnapping took place. The state-controlled media has yet to mention an event witnessed by dozens.

Stambolić's son reported him missing late on the same day as the kidnapping. Stambolić's wife hasn't stopped telephoning the police for updates. The police response?

"This is not a matter for the police," said a police spokesperson, who attributed the "alleged" kidnapping to a "*Mafiya* vendetta over business dealings."

Stambolić's family immediately shot back, explaining that since his retirement from public life his business dealings have been "totally above board. He was working to rebuild Yugoslavia, and he had no dealings with the *Mafiya*."

However, Stambolić had been considering a run against Slobodan Milošević in the upcoming presidential election. Stambolić reportedly put those plans on hold when a large group of opposition parties threw their support behind Stanimir Ateljević.

As admired and respected as Stambolić is, we cannot ignore the truth: Stambolić is responsible for where Milošević is today.

Slobodan Milošević met Ivan Stambolić at Belgrade University, and the two became fast friends. Stambolić was older and became a mentor to the man he often called "a promising young Bolshevik."

Stambolić himself was the son of ardent, well-connected Communist farmers, who set career goals for each of their sons: one would be a farmer; one would go to university; and one (Stambolić) would become an industrial worker. Stambolić faithfully followed his parents' plans. He became a worker and progressed upward in a machine tool factory and later a motor factory.

His duty to his parents was important to Stambolić, but he also had ambition. He switched to the night shift at the factory and went to Belgrade University Law School during the day. Milošević enrolled in law school the same time as Stambolić. The younger man became an admirer of Stambolić, a true worker.

Both men have said they took an instant liking to each other, but given Milošević's history, he was likely more attracted to Stambolić's family name and his family's strong ties to the Communist Party. Even if that were the case, for a long time, perhaps too long, Stambolić considered the friendship a deep one.

However, it wasn't deep enough for Milošević to share the truth of his personal life, namely the cause of his father's death.

After the elder Milošević gave a student a failing grade, that student killed himself. Filled with guilt, Milošević's father killed himself. Not long after, Milošević's closest uncle also committed suicide.

Then in his twenties, Milošević's penchant for covering up emerged early; he didn't attend his father's funeral, so no one would know. Nor did he share with his "dear friend" the reason for his own depression at the time. A decade after his father's suicide, Milošević's mother did so, too. Profilers of Milošević have concluded that this history of suicide in his family haunts Milošević to this day. Some allude to studies about the "hereditary" nature of suicide and suggest that Milošević fears that is his ultimate fate. Profilers site rumors that Milošević has had frequent and severe bouts of depression—something not acknowledged officially. Milošević's "tough guy" image might be a way for him to deal with those debilitating intervals.

But back to Ivan Stambolić.

With his law degree in hand and confident he'd fulfilled his parents' wish for him to be a worker,

Stambolić began his climb through the ranks of the Communist Party in Yugoslavia.

During his ascent, whenever he would vacate a position, he always had a recommendation for his replacement: his dear friend, Milošević. As Stambolić grew in power and prestige, he smoothed the way for Milošević, even when Party leaders weren't quite certain of Milošević's suitability. No one, however, doubted Stambolić.

During this time, Stambolić and his wife Katja were close with Milošević and his wife Mira. Gifts exchanged for birthdays. Holidays spent together. Regular backyard barbecues. All evincing a deep and abiding friendship.

Stambolić told others, "I love him like a brother."

Milošević made no similar statement but seemed satisfied with the relationship. Why not? Stambolić's upward mobility guaranteed the same path for Milošević, and Stambolić also had someone he trusted in the lower ranks of Party leadership. A perfect symbiosis.

After Tito's death, Stambolić became head of Serbia's Communist Party. Of course, he found a position as well for Milošević. Like Tito before him, Stambolić surrounded himself only with people he could trust, people he knew were loyal to him.

Indeed, Stambolić himself has said Milošević was one of only two people Stambolić trusted.

So doctrinaire was Milošević at this time, Stambolić gave him a nickname, "Little Lenin," and rewarded his loyalty by making him Belgrade's Communist Party Leader. Belgrade was capital not only of Serbia but of Yugoslavia.

This was a plum position, and Little Lenin filled it squarely, keeping the faithful in line with Marxist doctrine. He quickly identified dissidents and kept a list. He used the state-controlled media effectively, and people on that list were identified, scorned, and ridiculed, a practice that continues to this day.

Reform may have been where Milošević and Stambolić first began to drift apart politically. Right before becoming President of Serbia, Stambolić sent signals to the more liberal aspects in Yugoslavia that he was willing to hear them. Stambolić, with his extensive experience in real life and politics, understood the need to unify after Tito's death had put thoughts of independence into the minds and hearts of many of Yugoslavia's provinces.

Milošević, on the other hand, had recognized the benefits to him of divide and conquer. However, he stayed quiet about his plans because once Stambolić became president of Serbia, Milošević would become

Serbia's Communist Party Chief. In some ways, Milošević would be more powerful than Stambolić.

In truth, Milošević as astute enough to see that hitching himself to Stambolić's wagon, would only benefit Milošević, and he cultivated that friendship. Stambolić, no doubt flattered by Milošević's "loyalty," succumbed to the false charm and humility Milošević displayed. Stambolić always considered himself a worker first and surrounded himself with people of limited tastes. To that end, Milošević had, thus far, steered clear of corruption, had lived unpretentiously, and kept his own ambitions well-hidden.

That, of course, changed dramatically when Milošević became president.

On the night after Milošević's elevation to Serbian Communist Party chief, the two families of old friends celebrated. They all toasted Serbia's future, and Stambolić had no idea what Milošević had in store for him and for Yugoslavia.

If Stambolić has looked back in hindsight, that happy celebration would now be bittersweet.

To be continued.

Respond to author.

An excerpt from *Self-Inflicted Wounds:*
***Dangerous Truths* (Book 2)**

After a few, perfunctory stretches, Ivan Stambolić started his shuffle-jog toward the sports center. From an outdoor cafe, Mai watched his progress, savoring her coffee to allow some space to come between them.

But when Stambolić jogged past a white van, its engine started. He jogged ahead of it, and after a few moments it pulled from the parking space into the road, following Stambolić, moving slow enough to stay behind him.

Mai abandoned the coffee and hastened to catch up to Stambolić. The van's license plate was caked with mud, and the rear windows had been painted black.

Such an average vehicle could be the tool of the secret police or mercenary Russian assassins. At least some things in Yugoslavia were logical.

She had to increase her pace to a near-jog to close the gap with Stambolić. She brought out her mobile and speed-dialed Alexei.

"Bukharin," he answered.

"I need you here. They're moving in on Stambolić."

"Where are you exactly?"

"I was at that cafe, I'm about a block and a half from Stambolić, and he's taken a rest on a bench. A white van is tailing him. Can you get here?"

"Keep your distance. I'll be there in less than ten. Do not take them on by yourself."

Jesus Wept, she thought, and hung up. Mai drew her Beretta, keeping it down by her thigh. In a full run now, she closed on Stambolić. She looked at the van and could see the driver's face in the side mirror. Kolya. He must have seen her, too. The van sped up, coming abreast of Stambolić, the side door sliding open.

Mai brought the Beretta up and fired into the open van door. A definite yelp of pain came from inside.

"Stambolić!" she screamed as she ran toward him.

Stambolić turned toward her, his mouth forming an "o" when he saw her gun. A man dressed all in black stepped down from the van.

"Police," said the man, "get in the van."

Stambolić shook his head and stood up from the bench. The other man drew a gun, and Mai stopped, gauntleted her gun in both hands, and double-tapped the man in the chest. With no body armor, he dropped to the sidewalk, a rivulet of blood trickling toward the gutter.

"Stambolić!" Mai shouted. "Come with me! Now!"

Two more men emerged from the van and grabbed Stambolić. Gunfire came from the driver side of the van, the bullets digging divots in the sidewalk in front of Mai.

EuroScene
Dateline: Belgrade

Where is Ivan Stambolić?
Part 2
(Belgrade Correspondent)

Serbian nationalism drove the definitive wedge between Ivan Stambolić and his "brother" Slobodan Milošević. By his own admission, Stambolić never saw the break coming.

In the mid-1980s when popular novels and music extolled a greater Serbia, Stambolić and the Communist Party maintained Tito's version of socialism. As a good Communist, Stambolić was a true believer in Tito's "Brotherhood and Unity" vision and continued it as an homage. Milošević either never believed in it or abandoned it later for his own purpose, but his silence Stambolić interpreted as support.

At this point in his career, Milošević's views on Yugoslavian brotherhood and unity were evolving. Known only to his wife, Mira and likely encouraged by her, he had set as his political and personal objective the creation of a Greater Serbia. Not one among equals but one above all others, of Serbians, for Serbians, and by any means necessary.

And Stambolić unwittingly gave Milošević that means and certainly the opportunity to become a nationalist hero.

When Serbians complained they would be forced to flee the "sacred" province of Kosovo because the majority ethnic Albanians there were mistreating them, Stambolić sent his most trusted associate to Kosovo to remind the Serbians they were all Yugoslavians. Milošević's prepared speech, drafted for Stambolić, contained words to calm and assure Kosovar Serbians. However, the crowd of unruly Serbians assembled at the Hall of Culture in Pristina had another idea.

Pressing in on Milošević and his entourage, the crowd turned angry, and Milošević knew the high-level words of oneness in his prepared speech would only elevate the propensity for violence, and he would be right in the middle of it. He opted to speak to them off the cuff, at that time not his strong suit.

Being the chair of Serbia's Communist Party, he started with, of course, the party line: "The Party will solve this."

The crowd's anger increased. "But they are beating us!" someone in the crowd yelled, his sentiment taken up by others. The assembled Serbians shouted a litany of offenses aimed at them because they were Serbians.

What followed was a minor but seminal moment in history, one historians write books about. With his best strategist by his side, Milošević replied exactly as he needed to, a response that made him the savior of Serbians everywhere.

"No one will ever beat you again!"

Unbridled cheers, fawning admiration can be heady for an insecure person, and Milošević bathed in the attention. Moreover, it inspired him. His next words, though spoken in 1987, he has repeated in some form wherever conflict arose. "You must stay here! Your land is here. Yugoslavia does not exist without Kosovo! Yugoslavia—and Serbia—will not give up Kosovo!"

Back in Belgrade, Stambolić was shocked at this display of nationalism from a trusted comrade, from his brother. Stambolić had sent Milošević to put out the fire, not pour gasoline on it. Members of the Serbian Communist Party, who had only voted for Milošević because Stambolić wanted it, pushed back with Stambolić, reminding him that Tito had eschewed the cult of personality and broken from Stalin because of that. What they'd seen in Kosovo was the beginning of the Milošević cult of personality; it needed to be stopped before it spread beyond a few hundred Serbs in Pristina.

But before Milošević arrived back in Belgrade, newspapers had already published poems about him as a hero of Serbia, letters extolled the "handsome young speaker" and mentioned how the setting sun fell "on his brushed hair."

All that went to the head beneath that telegenically coiffed hair.

"Kosovo!" became a battle cry for all Serbs, and it became Milošević's personal issue. His circle of friends who now wanted to attach themselves to his rising star used the media to his advantage. Someone in his circle traced Milošević's family tree back to the Battle of Kosovo in 1389. When Serbs read that in state-controlled publications, it convinced them Milošević was the right man for Serbia.

But there was one obstacle in the way.

Milošević needed to dump his oldest friend.

Politicians are politicians, after all, and they heeded the way the people took to Milošević's declaration, "No one will ever beat you again!" They rallied to his side, attaching themselves to his ascendance. On some level, Stambolić must have been proud to see his protege come into his own. What he didn't know was that his beloved and media-savvy brother had orchestrated attacks on Stambolić in the controlled press. Media outlets questioned Stambolić's patriotism and his Party loyalty when he didn't vocally agree with Milošević and when he disagreed with the calling of a special session of the Communist Party Central Committee.

Who called the special session? Why, the Party chief, of course. Slobodan Milošević had because of a minor event at an army barracks in Paracin, Serbia.

There, an ethnic Albanian conscript shot other soldiers in his barracks, killing four, wounding six. One of the four dead was a Serb, but the main, state-controlled newspaper, *Politika*, played it up as a massacre of Serbs by non-Serbs and denounced it as an act of separatism against Yugoslavia. The public also didn't know the shooter had been declared deranged before being drafted. He heard voices, people were told, voices telling him to kill Serbs. Urged on by Milošević, the press built up the incident until people were in a frenzy. Tens of thousands attended the funeral of the single Serb fatality and screamed for revenge.

Stambolić tried to stem the rising tide of intolerance with a hasty press conference, one arranged so quickly someone forgot to notify Milošević, who caught it on television. After viewing the presser, Milošević was furious. He'd spent this effort in whipping up the populace, and here was a man Serbs respected trying to calm everything. In Stambolić's reaction, Milošević found the final thread to weave Stambolić's downfall.

Milošević remained quiet, in the background, and didn't overtly dispute Stambolić; for all intents and purposes still the loyal and faithful protege. All the while his friends in the press and his own wife intensified their attacks against Stambolić up to the Central Committee special session, which Milošević insisted be televised.

Even then, Stambolić believed he and Milošević were friends, brothers. He turned to his friend for reassurance about the special session, and Milošević didn't falter. Milošević assured Stambolić, "There is no problem in it for you."

This Central Committee special session was an insight into Milošević's character. He'd set the meeting up to go his way. He'd carefully stacked the deck, cemented alliances, made promises, assured the support of the generals and the police. Then, he sat back and listened to the speeches in silence.

Speaker after speaker denounced Stambolić, the seasoned, committed Communist, for straying from Tito's ideals. They all seemed to forget or ignore Stambolić shared those ideals: Brotherhood and unity for Yugoslavia, not a Serbian Yugoslavia, not a nationalistic Serbia above all others.

This was the point where Stambolić's long friendship ended, but he still couldn't see it or denied it. His response only fed the disillusionment with him.

"Let us sit down over coffee or lemonade and overcome our differences. I know you, and I will not accept that we cannot find humane solutions. I will not accept that." Stambolić looked to his friend, his brother for support.

"This question cannot be minimized by describing it as if we are two children having a squabble," said Milošević or words to this effect.

But Stambolić maintained his desire to be reasonable and appealed to Milošević to bring people together and not create divisions. It was an impassioned plea, from one old friend to another.

Party Chief Milošević wouldn't look at his friend and merely said, "Next speaker."

Stambolić had no choice but to remove himself from the podium.

This public humiliation wasn't enough for Miloše-vić. He had allies in the Party circulate a false letter they said Stambolić had sent them to pressure them into voting for Stambolić's positions. Milošević "reluctantly" went to Stambolić with a copy of the letter, hesitant to voice his "concerns." The meeting was private, but Milošević had managed to distribute the letter widely, and the wording made it appear Stambolić was openly encouraging dissent against the Communist Party.

Stambolić finally accepted reality. Later, he would refer to Milošević's "performance" as "Oscar-worthy…. When I saw Milošević's face, I thought the Russians had invaded."

Stambolić knew he was done for when Milošević issued a public statement wherein he stated he suspected Stambolić had been manipulated.

He had. By a man he'd "loved like a brother."

Three months later, the Communist Party removed Stambolić as President of Serbia, an act more symbolic than anything. Stambolić's power had ceased the day Milošević had swept him from the podium with two words.

Several weeks later, Stambolić's twenty-four-year-old daughter died in an automobile accident, and an editorial in a state-run publication, *Ekspres*, stated, "His [Stambolić's] seed in its roots must be crushed."

In his grief and now suspecting his daughter had been murdered, Stambolić reached out one final time to his so-called friend. He told Milošević the editorial had been tasteless.

"I had nothing to do with that. We have freedom of the press," was the reply.

As far as anyone knows, that was their last conversation. Years later, Stambolić discussed now-President Milošević with friends. With 20/20 hindsight he said, "He'll use anyone, then throw them away."

Stambolić went into banking after his ouster, settled in a nice suburb of Belgrade where many foreign embassies housed their staffs. He was recognized by many during his daily jogs in the neighborhood. On August 25, 2000, as he jog-shuffled along never too far from his apartment, a white van followed him. Witnesses told the police this.

Other witnesses reported that "arrogant, crew-cut young men" had been hanging out near the route Stambolić ran every day. Secret police, people assumed, spying on the diplomats in the neighborhood. They looked the other way, because that is what you do when the secret police are watching.

As usual, midway through his jog, Stambolić approached a bench across the street from a popular restaurant, where he would take a breather before resuming his jog. The parking lot attendant recognized him and told police, "He is a fixture here. We see him every day."

The attendant also said a white van pulled up, blocking his view of Stambolić.

When the van pulled away, the bench was empty.

Respond to author.

CHAPTER 14

An excerpt from *Self-Inflicted Wounds:*
And Justice for All **(Book 3)**

The body armor made Vojislav Ranovesić sweat. *The sweat made him itch in places he'd be embarrassed to scratch in public. The itch made him scowl, and that scowl held back those for whom his police uniform still had power. Despite his confident exterior, Ranovesić wondered how his outnumbered Belgrade police—since the federal police wouldn't help—could hold back a crowd intent on revolution.*

Slobodan Milošević had lost an election. By the numbers. Of course, he couldn't accept that, however, insisting that his opponent, though clearly ahead, didn't have a majority over fifty percent. Therefore, Milošević was still president.

The people were having none of it, and in the almost two weeks since the hastily called elections, the crowds in the streets had grown to the point where Ranovesić thought the entire country had come to Belgrade.

There was the inevitable tear gas, and that made them retreat. For a while. Many of the demonstrators, wet handkerchiefs over their noses and mouths, threw the canisters back at the police. One by one, Ranovesić's men had left the police line to join family and friends among the demonstrators. Now, a thin line of Belgrade police in riot gear was all that stood between the parliament building and citizens demanding the overthrow of Milošević. Ranovesić was part of that line. He'd started his career as a street policeman. Unlike other secretariat commanders in Serbia, he would be here with his men; their fate would be his.

He only hoped Anja and his daughters would understand if he paid the price with his life.

This mob of farmers and miners and doctors and lawyers and housewives shouted not only for Milošević to go but for that elusive and ever-evolving form of government, democracy. The world had considered Tito's Yugoslavia the most democratic of the Soviet satellites. But the Yugoslavs, from a nation created on paper and held together by Josip Broz's formidable will and his oppressive secret police, knew if you were within Tito's circle, a member of his party, you had all the freedom you wanted. Then, Tito was mortal after all, his death followed by rotating presidencies and culminating in Slobodan Milošević and unimaginable hardship.

Ranovesić had become a policeman under Tito and lasted through Milošević by staying neutral but making that look like commitment. Some in this crowd would consider that as much a crime as tyranny. They didn't understand that, like them, he had to worry about rent money, clothes for his children, and his spouse's government job, which could have been quickly taken away if he hadn't done his duty.

Now, here you stand, Voja, he thought, committed to protecting Milošević's parliament against a mob who insisted Milošević was finished, who called for Ateljević to be the new president because, can you imagine, he got the most votes. Ranovesić would protect this building because this was his city and it was his job.

His heart, however, didn't have to be in it.

☙ ☙

EuroScene
Dateline: Belgrade

Is He Really Finished?
(Belgrade Correspondent)

CAMPAIGNING for the hastily called elections is in full force. The carefully orchestrated demonstrations for Milošević get shown on state television, where the camera angles intimate large, adoring crowds. If you look closer, you see the same group of people from different angles.

What people don't see on state television are the huge numbers at campaign rallies for Stanimir Ateljević. Polls taken by independent entities show Ateljević well in the lead. Milošević's polls show the opposite. Those in the know say Milošević's smiles at his rallies are a mask, that he's running scared.

Unfortunately, backing Milošević into an electoral corner is not good for the health of opposition candidates, but so far Ateljević has not been targeted by the roving band of thugs everyone knows are secret police. If Ateljević fears for his life, he doesn't show it either. His public appearances are without obvious security, only his supporters as his protection. Recently, when someone struck him with a rock at a rally in Kosovo, he held his handkerchief to the wound and finished his speech.

Aside from the fear of police brutality, the campaign exhibits typical behavior you would find in England or America. As quickly as "He is Finished" signs go up, the secret police pull them down, only to have more spring up a block away.

However, this activity keeps the police too busy to beat up anyone.

One significant difference in this campaign from the election several years before when Milošević set aside the results as "tainted" and declared himself the winner is that European observers are everywhere, even if they weren't requested by the government. They are truly only observers, and they won't be allowed at the polls on election day. Their presence, however, fuels optimism among European powers that this particular election might have some semblance of democracy.

The people, however, because of recent history, never set aside their skepticism.

"Ateljević may get more votes," said a miner holding up a "He is Finished!" poster at an Ateljević rally. "But we all know that somehow Slobodan will be the winner, probably by his own declaration."

Police and army support for Milošević fuels the people's cynicism. They will go to the polls and vote in an election which offers them a real choice, but they have a sneaking suspicion the outcome has already been decided. Still, they hope they're wrong.

In the midst of the campaign, the recent string of murders of prominent officials, the "friends of Slobo" murders as some media outlets called them, have stopped. Quite a few cases are still unsolved, as is one kidnapping, that of Ivan Stambolić, who might have been the one man who could defeat Milošević without question.

Mention Stambolić to people, and they shake their heads, some unable to speak, some with tears in their eyes.

After constant prompting from Stambolić's family and supporters, the police issued a statement: Stambolić had been arrested for anti-government activities and treachery.

When pressed for details, that became, "Oh, he's only in protective custody, and for his safety we can't tell you where."

Stambolić, the working man's hero, the scion of an old Communist family, the inadvertent creator of the Butcher of the Balkans, is missed in Belgrade, where his daily jogs were a common sight. His modest lifestyle compared to Milošević's $3,000 suits and $20,000 watches is noted.

If the Yugoslavian people seem resigned to a preordained Milošević victory, the rest of Europe is jumpy about it. No one outside of Yugoslavia wants another Milošević presidency, but some European governments have worried that if Milošević loses, Milošević and his wife will suffer the fate of the Ceausescus, that Milošević and Markovic will be shot live on state television.

"That won't happen," said the same Ateljević-supporting miner. "We want to see him on trial, here in Yugoslavia. We are not Romanians."

Even in determining the fate of their dictator, the fractious ethnic tenets of the Balkans emerges.

Milošević appears before hand-selected, sympathetic audiences. Little girls in Serbian folk dresses give him bouquets. He waves, that so-hesitant smile on his face. His wife looks at him adoringly. He doesn't seem to break a sweat. He speaks in a calm voice, and the audience applauds without prompting at his planned pauses.

Ateljević shouts his speeches until his throat is raw. Hands reach for him, dislodging his tie, mussing his hair. Often, the stink of a day's travel around the country in a close car wafts from his body. He remains invigorated.

Is he the right man to be the next president of Yugoslavia? The West seems to think so, but they forget he, too, is a nationalist and one of the most outspoken critics of NATO's bombardment last year. His speeches are full of criticism for Milošević, to be sure, but he saves some of his harshest words for the head of NATO, the British prime minister, and the American president.

Ateljević has, at least, an open mind. He can be dealt with. An ethnically pure, Serbian Yugoslavia will not be his priority if he is elected. Getting gasoline and heating oil for the upcoming winter are. Restoring the infrastructure still in ruins from smart bombs is. Renewing the faith of a people so long turned in on themselves is at the top of his agenda.

Whether Milošević is truly finished may still be up for grabs, but there is one certainty. Milošević continues to dwell in a past of imagined Serbian glory. Ateljević is the future.

Respond to Author.

CHAPTER 15

**An excerpt from *Self-Inflicted Wounds:
And Justice for All* (Book 3)**

There is a member of the secret police—and don't ask me which one because it's all a mess now—wants to make a deal with you."

"What does he have to deal?"

"He only told me vague things, but I knew it would interest you."

"Like what?"

"A connection between a certain person currently in custody in The Hague and the political murders you stopped last year."

Mai shook her head and switched to Russian, "Vy ponimaete eta lovushka."

"No trap," Oleg said.

"How sure are you of that?"

"He has a young daughter with leukemia and needs money for a bone marrow transplant in Vienna."

Mai raised a skeptical eyebrow.

Oleg shrugged again and said, "I have looked into his eyes. He loves his child."

"His price?"

"You can afford it."

"Still, what's he asking?"

"Fifty thousand dollars."

"Jesus Wept, I don't want the holy grail."

"Maiya, please," Oleg said, crossing himself three times, "do not blaspheme."

"How do I know I'll get something worthwhile?"

"He said he had proof, but, fuck, Maiya, that's the price of a car for your granddaughter. Are you bargaining with the life of a child?"

"I don't know why it surprises me when Russians get sentimental at the oddest times. Where is the bastard?"

"In a private room in the back. Number three. I will watch from my office."

"And you were so sure it wasn't a trap."

A final shrug and Oleg replied, "Like you said, Russians can be sentimental."

EuroScene
Dateline: Belgrade

Tumbling Pigeons
(Belgrade Correspondent)

IN EUROPE, there is a breed of pigeon known for its aerobatics. In flight, they somersault or flip in the air, appear to tumble about. These antics are being used to describe a new breed, as it were, in Balkan politics.

"Tumbling pigeons" are those who, before the street revolution that assured Stanimir Ateljević's victory over Slobodan Milošević, were staunch, often fawning Milošević supporters. Now that he's out and Ateljević is in, they declare, "We won!"

Often the sardonic response is, "'We?' Before, you wanted nothing to do with us."

Those pigeons are tumbling for economic and survival reasons, and they come from all walks of previous Milošević-support life: businessmen, police, government workers, state-run media, soldiers.

Turncoats are not new to Yugoslavia, but these sudden conversions are met with skepticism.

A Belgrade zookeeper is upset that "tumbling pigeons" now describes those who so abruptly changed sides. "The pigeons tumble because that's what's in their instincts. They know no better.

Humans, however, know exactly what they're doing. It's unfair to the pigeons," he said.

When state television "tumbled" and landed solidly behind Ateljević, when the police showed similar support, it was inevitable that Milošević would go out with a whimper and not a bang. In the end, the police and the army, for a change, sided with the people and their choice, Ateljević.

Pigeons have tumbled everywhere except for the Serbs in Kosovo, despite Ateljević's nationalist reassurances there.

Ateljević has also won support for announcing an amnesty for political prisoners. Determining who is truly jailed for his or her politics and who isn't could be problematic. No one wants to see the prisons emptied en masse, especially when every murderer and rapist could declare themselves political prisoners.

There is one legacy of his predecessor Ateljević seems content to ignore.

Ivan Stambolić remains missing.

It's become clear he wasn't arrested; he isn't in "protective custody;" no one can identify precisely where he's being held. This led an Ateljević spokesperson to declare, "Stambolić is not in custody anywhere in Yugoslavia."

People want to know where he is, and no answer is forthcoming.

Is his fate the same as a judge who went missing right after the election and whose body surfaced some time later at the point where the Danube and the Sava merge?

A policeman said, "The rivers have always been a good dumping ground for bodies you don't want to be found for a while."

Stambolić has been missing for months, since right before the election. Both the old government and the new have turned a deaf ear to his family.

Ateljević refuses to extradite Milošević, indicted for war crimes, to stand trial at the World Court. He's convinced that, as a deliberating body, it is prejudiced against Serbs since it's indicted so many of them. (Croats and Bosnians have also been indicted, but because Serbia had the army and police and all those paramilitary units, more Serbs have been indicted than other ethnicities.)

To forestall criticism from the west and the drying up of the lifelines connected with his election, Ateljević has said Milošević will be tried in Yugoslavia. For corruption. Not crimes against humanity.

Ateljević may be worried about the impartiality of a World Court trial for Milošević, but others, like Zoran Djindjic, prime minister of Serbia, fear there'll be no trial at all since the judiciary is still solidly pro-Milošević. A chief judge in Belgrade has vowed that

Milošević will not be tried for anything so long as this judge is in charge.

Another judge who challenged that declaration disappeared soon after, found four days later in his car and shot multiple times. Suicide, said the police.

Or have the political murders started again?

Authorities point to Dutch "mercenaries" in custody since the election for plotting to kill Milošević and hint they were responsible for all the recent friends of Slobo murders. They've never been charged with any crime, and the police refuse to answer when asked what crimes they are being held for. One man arrested for killing Arkan a year ago has recanted his confession and claims he was framed.

Perhaps nothing much has changed in Yugoslavia.

The average person doesn't pay much attention to those unsolved murders. The focus is on rebuilding and ferreting out corruption, admirable goals to be sure. Ateljević is working hard to meet the needs of his people. One hopes for all his people.

But western governments who supported him as a candidate remind him their promised investments in Yugoslavia may be in question unless he does something about Milošević.

Each day, a government spokesperson assures Milošević's arrest is "imminent," but so far nothing. And Milošević remains in charge of the Socialist Party because he is a free man. Thousands of people all over Yugoslavia lie uneasy in their graves—mass and individual—because of that.

There is some grim satisfaction that most of his allies have abandoned him. Even one of his children fled to Moscow after the street demonstrations assured Ateljević's victory. His most loyal supporter remains, as always, his wife.

Many of the people who would have stayed the course with him, who rose in power as he did, are dead—killed over the past decade and whose murders for the most part remain unsolved. The police have other priorities now.

Unless someone, somewhere, admits to any of it, it could forever remain a mystery who killed the friends of Slobodan Milošević. And why.

Respond to author.

The End

July 2020
Staunton, Virginia

Welcome to Belgrade, book one
of *Self-Inflicted Wounds*, releases on October 1, 2020.

ACKNOWLEDGEMENTS

Thanks to Jennie Coughlin, journalist extraordinaire, who read an early version of the *Self-Inflicted Wounds* trilogy this reader magnet is based on and declared my scattering of news stories (created by me based on my research) throughout the narrative too distracting from the story. I tend to take her advice because in addition to being a superb journalist, she's an incredible writer and beta reader for me.

So, I had all these vignettes I'd deleted. What to do with them, since I felt they did explain the atmosphere in Yugoslavia in 2000?

Thanks second to Audrey Hughey, my marketing consultant, who'd already introduced me to the concept of a reader magnet for an upcoming work of fiction. She suggested I use those vignettes as a reader magnet. The first draft was disjointed and almost incomprehensible, and she said, "Well, use a pertinent excerpt from the trilogy before each one."

Duh. Now you see why I have her in my fold.

Thanks, finally, to the usual suspects: members of my various writing groups and classmates from the Tinker Mountain Writers Workshops and Retreats.

ABOUT THE AUTHOR

 P. A. Duncan is a former aviation safety official and minor bureaucrat but one with an overactive imagination. A graduate of Madison College (now James Madison University) with degrees in History and Political Science, she lives and writes in the beautiful Shenandoah Valley of Virginia. There, she also watches NASCAR, cheers on the New York Yankees, and delights in spoiling grandchildren.

Her award-winning fiction has been published in numerous literary journals and anthologies. She is the author of several novels, novellas, novelettes, and many short stories.

Follow me here:

Amazon Author Page: amazon.com/
author/phyllisduncan

BookBub: https://www.bookbub.com/profile/p-a-
duncan

Facebook Author Page: www.
faebook.com/unspywriter

Facebook Reader Group: www.facebook.com/
group/RealSpies

Goodreads: http://bit.ly/GRPADuncan

Instagram: www:instagram.com/paduncan1

Newsletter Sign-up: http://bit.ly/SecretBriefings

Pinterest: www.pinterest.com/paduncan01

Twitter: www.twitter.com/unspywriter

Website/Blog: www.unexpectedpaths.com

ALSO BY P. A. DUNCAN

Find all of the author's work at

amazon.com/author/phyllisduncan

Short Story Collections

Blood Vengeance, 2012

Spy Flash, 2012

The Better Spy, 2015

Spy Flash II, 2016

Spy Flash III: The Moscow Rules, coming Spring 2021

Short Story Singles/Reader Magnets

"A Visit from Grandfather Frost," 2017, published in the
Skyline 2019 Anthology

"The Broader Concerns of All Humanity," 2018,

(A Perfect Hatred: End Times)

"What You Have to Do," 2018,

(A Perfect Hatred: Bad Company)

"A Case of Mistaken Identity," 2019,

(A Perfect Hatred: Descending Spiral)

"Settling Scores," 2019,

(A Perfect Hatred: Collateral Damage)

Novelettes

A Face in the Crowd, 2017, sequel to *A War of Deception*

Novellas

The Yellow Scarf, 2015

"REAL SPIES, REAL LIVES" PODCAST

Listen on Anchor, Apple Podcasts, Breaker,
Google Podcasts, iTunes, Overcast, RadioPublic,
and Spotify.

DON'T FORGET THE REVIEW

I'm sure you've heard all the cliches, and I'm a writer, so allow me to indulge in a few. Reviews are a writer's life's blood. We live for them. We weep with joy over the good ones. We express (inwardly) righteous indignation at the bad ones. How else would we improve as writers without them?

Bottom line? All those cliches are reality for us. I will continue to write whether people love my writing or hate it, but a few kind words on Amazon, Goodreads, or BookBub is all you have to do to make me smile.

Read on,

P. A. Duncan

CHAPTER ONE
"Small Talk"

Belgrade, Yugoslavia
Belgrade Intercontinental Hotel
January 2000

From the corner of his eye, the doorman saw the large, black Mercedes approach. Lights from the city's New Year's decorations reflected off its mirror finish, almost brighter than the lights themselves. Straightening from his slouch against the wall, he rubbed his gloveless hands together to warm them. The Mercedes stopped before him, and he murmured a quick prayer. The car had no dents or scratches, no obvious bullet holes; the possibility of a decent tip chased the cold away.

He hustled to open the door, and a woman emerged. She ignored his offered hand. She wore sunglasses in the dark, and her dour mouth was a straight line. His hopes for that tip took a bit of a dive, but something touched his palm. Closing his fingers around what rested there, he recognized aristocracy in the subtlety of her gesture.

The doorman shut the car's door and jogged to get ahead of the woman. He held the hotel's ornate door open for her, and a second pressure in his hand lifted his spirits. To acknowledge her generosity would be obsequious. He murmured, "Good evening," as he pocketed both tips. She slid past him without eye contact. The Mercedes pulled ahead so it no longer blocked the entrance and sat, idling, its exhaust a billowing cloud in the chill air.

THE LOBBY OFFERED ALL the usual activities of a major hotel in a European capital city. To escape the weather, a uniformed policeman sat at a table in the lounge, facing the entrance. He nursed a cup of coffee and watched one of the waitresses on her travels about the room.

Their body language proclaiming their interest in each other, a man and a woman sat at the opposite end of the lounge from the policeman.

People checked in. Others strolled about, entering or leaving the lounge, perhaps using the lobby to elude the frigid night.

Curious faces turned toward the door when a blast of cold air accompanied the woman's entrance. They all resumed their previous engagements after determining their disinterest. She wasn't dressed like a *kurva*, looking for her next john, but in her all-black attire, she blended well with any other person who'd be out and about on the streets of Belgrade in the middle of the night.

The policeman's eyes stayed on her longest, but when she mounted the three steps to a private alcove in the lounge, he quickly looked away.

The elevated alcove allowed its occupant to see everything and everyone in the lobby. The better furniture was there: leather sofas, plush chairs. Most of them were empty.

One man sat in the largest of the chairs, a perimeter of unoccupied seats and a semi-circle of bodyguards around him. With no hint of expression, the bodyguards watched her approach, eyes on her hands, their hands inside coats, ready for their weapons if she reached for hers.

The seated man narrowed his eyes at her, a hint of a smile on his mouth. Željko Ražnatović, aka Arkan, wasn't a tall man, but he loomed as a nationalist hero to Serbs and a monster to Bosnian Muslims. His physical presence sans uniform was nondescript. The cut of the expensive suit hid his slight paunch. His close-cropped hair had started to recede, but the cut was from an expensive stylist, no doubt. He dressed like the "simple businessman" he proclaimed to be.

He attributed his wealth to a string of ice cream parlors and internet cafes, but in addition to having been one of Belgrade's top ethnic cleansers, he was a leader in Belgrade's underworld. More likely that fortune came from selling tax-free cigarettes, bootleg videos and CDs, and contraband gasoline. His bland, almost boyish face was a familiar one at the hotel, where he sometimes conducted his public meetings.

When the woman reached him, he stood.

His men shifted closer when she removed and pocketed her sunglasses, revealing her hard-set, uncompromising face. Ražnatović's eyes roamed her body, hidden behind a long, leather coat. His gaze settled on the twin streaks of white in her hair, one at each temple, markers of having been his prisoner eight years before.

He smiled, waved his men back to the shadows around the bar, and put his fate in her hands.

☙ ☙

KEEPING her face expressionless was an exercise in control, but when Arkan moved to greet her Serbian style—kisses on both cheeks—she backed up a step.

"Please," Arkan said, "if we do not greet each other the right way, people will suspect this is a personal meeting, and neither of us wants that."

She stiffened when his hands gripped her upper arms, but she gave no reaction when he kissed her cheeks, his lips lingering. With a silent vow to scrub her face after she left, she returned the gesture.

Arkan motioned to the chair next to his, and she sat, crossing her legs at the knee and letting her gloved hands rest in her lap. Arkan sat and summoned a waitress with a flick of his fingers.

"You want something to drink?" he asked. After her silence, he added, "Remember this is to look like business."

"Whiskey. Neat."

Arkan told the waitress what to bring, handed her a U.S. twenty-dollar bill, and waved off the change.

"You take much convincing to have simple meeting," Arkan said in his passable English.

"I considered the source."

Arkan's boisterous laugh was for show, to demonstrate to anyone watching their encounter was nothing more than two business associates well met.

"I am merely a businessman, nothing more."

"Yes, that reads well in the state press," she replied. Her dark eyes became flints. In Serbian, she added, "You're a fucking butcher. Nothing more. I'm here. Talk."

Even the fake humor left his eyes. "I remember it is always so intense with you. No small talk. I pity your husband. He must never get to be on top when you fuck."

"Why am I here?"

Arkan's sigh of exasperation was as affected as his laughter. "Small talk. We must do small talk, then, we drink, perhaps dinner, seal deal, as you say."

She didn't reply, and the silence expanded between them. A smile hovering at his lips, his eyes watched her face for a reaction.

"How old is that child now?" he asked. "The one you so rigorously protected inside you when you were my...guest. Seven? Eight? That was in 'ninety-two. Eight this year, am I right? Was it a boy or a girl?"

She was glad the look she gave him made a bodyguard step closer, but Arkan held up a hand.

"Oh," he murmured, "there must have been an unfortunate accident. That is too bad because, of course, you are too old for another."

She stood, and the bodyguards, all of them, rushed toward her.

Again, Arkan's casual lifting of a hand stopped them.

"My apologies," he said, "for bringing up bad memories." He didn't bother to put any forced sincerity behind it. "Sit. Hear what I have to say."

She looked at the bodyguards. Arkan again waved his hand at them, and they backed away.

She waited long enough to sit that he wouldn't think she'd obeyed him. She'd had more than enough of that eight years ago.

Welcome to Belgrade will be available for preorder in September and launches on October 1, 2020. Keep an eye out for the details on the author's Facebook Group, website, or newsletter. See the "Author's Social Media" page above.

Made in the USA
Columbia, SC
14 August 2020